BRIDGERS 1: THE LURE OF INFINITY

STAN C. SMITH

SAFETREK

ISBN-13: 978-1987592887

ISBN-10: 1987592883

To those who see wonder in places untrodden by human feet.

THE LURE OF INFINITY

By their nature, intelligent species cannot resist the lure of infinite worlds.

INFINITY FOWLER

1

INCOMING

July 16

THIRTY-SIX HOURS CAN FEEL like a long time—even longer if you're being hunted. Infinity Fowler pressed her naked body into the dirt and dead leaves of the forest floor. Small insects began biting her skin, but she was too exhausted to care. She thrust out her right hand, palmed the bare scalp of the tourist beside her, and forced his head down until his cheek was in the dirt.

"Stay down!" she hissed.

The tourist nodded. His eyes were wide, but he had a slight grin on his face, as if he were pleased to be getting his money's worth.

Just beyond the tourist lay Infinity's partner, Hornet. He was staring out through the low vegetation, his black body blending in with the shadows of the forest floor. Infinity cursed silently, regretting that she hadn't taken the time to smear mud on her and the tourist's pale skin.

Hornet's muscles went rigid. He had heard something. Infinity turned slowly and gazed through the sparse saplings they had chosen for cover. She heard something faintly disturbing the leaves, perhaps a hundred feet out. At first she thought it was a squirrel or a bird. But a large body—even a cautious, deliberate one—created a subtly distinct sound. The creatures were coming.

She applied more pressure to the tourist's scalp, a signal to stay still. The guy had been willing to work hard and even fight. But he was an idiot, and he was already bruised and bleeding from half a dozen wounds. Infinity and Hornet would be docked for every one of them. If they made it back alive.

The sound of crunching leaves was getting closer. If the creatures were moving through the forest randomly, there was a chance they'd pass by without incident. But more likely the creatures were tracking them, following the disturbed leaf litter. Infinity and Hornet had already underestimated the creatures' skill and perseverance more than once.

Fight or flight? This was the fundamental dilemma every bridger was trained to face. And Infinity was a good bridger. The sun was low on the horizon, so their thirty-six hours had to be almost up. But how many minutes were left? She had no way to know for sure. If they ran now, they might gain a few more minutes. Or maybe not. If she and Hornet fought and won, they might gain another hour or more. If they fought and lost, the tourist might have a better chance to get away, as long as he started running now before the creatures were within sight. She knew what she had to do.

She released the tourist's head. "Run," she whispered. "Go as far as you can. Don't stop. Hiding won't help. Go now."

He frowned. "No."

She grabbed his head again and tried digging her fingernails into his scalp, but the dead tissue of her nails had been stripped away while bridging to this world. She snarled. "Run!"

"I'm not going to miss this."

She stared at him, seething.

"Incoming," Hornet whispered.

Infinity looked through the brush. It was too late—the creatures were close. She saw two of them creeping among the trees. They were no more than five feet tall, and their faces were butt-ugly, with ape brows and low, sloping foreheads. Neanderthals, most likely, or whatever Neanderthals had become in the last 100,000 years. Weird tattooed or painted patterns made their faces look menacing. They wore tight pants made of woven fabric that looked stretchable. Their upper bodies were wrapped tightly with dozens of colored cords, some stretched over each shoulder and some wrapped around the abdomen. Their long, blond hair was drawn into ponytails behind their heads, and a melon-sized pouch clung to the side of each man's waist.

They may have been short, but their bodies were thick. They had already proven to be powerful, and they could run like goddamn cheetahs, at least for a few seconds. Each of them held a weapon in his hand, an atlatl-type thing with a fifteen-inch wooden handle that allowed them to throw heavy, foot-long darts carved from stone. These creatures were formidable, and Infinity wouldn't underestimate the bastards again.

One of the creatures pointed at the ground, probably at blood drops or some other sign the humans had left behind. The creature spoke—the first time Infinity had heard them talk. His voice was higher and more feminine than she had expected, and the language included a lot of pops and clicks. Both of them erupted with what could only have been laughter. The bastards were having fun.

The creatures stopped. They sniffed the air. Infinity gripped the primitive spear lying beside her. Within seconds she'd be fighting for her life.

She turned to the tourist and whispered, "Hornet and I will try to kill them. Bridge-back is close. Only minutes. If they kill *us*, run."

The tourist just grinned and nodded. He should have been pissing himself.

The creatures were looking straight at them. They had heard her talking. Infinity glanced at Hornet, and their eyes met. No point in trying to be silent now.

"We go to them," she said. This would give the tourist the best chance to run.

Hornet nodded.

They jumped to their feet and charged. Naked. Weaponless except for crude spears made from saplings sharpened by rubbing the tips against a rock.

The creatures looked at each other and smiled, and then both of them let out high-pitched screams. They raised their atlatls to launch their stone darts.

Infinity kept running, but she dodged to the side to put a tree between herself and the creatures. She intentionally carried her spear in both hands to make them think she planned to wield it as a close-quarters weapon. But when the creatures were within ten yards, she darted from behind the tree and launched the weapon, surprising them. From the corner of her eye, she saw Hornet carry out the same maneuver from behind another tree.

But the creatures launched their darts at the same moment the humans left their cover. Infinity dove for the ground and a stone dart whistled over her.

"Jesus!" Hornet mumbled. He was sitting on the ground clutching his shoulder. A dart was protruding from his back, having almost passed through his dense body.

There was no time to check on him. Infinity got to her feet and closed in on the creatures. One of them had staggered back, a spear through his thigh. The other dropped his atlatl and pulled two weapons from the pouch at his side—a curved stone knife for his left hand and a heavy axe for his right. Ignoring his injured companion, he smiled at Infinity and gyrated the two weapons in a complex, almost artistic pattern, weaving them back and forth expertly. Probably a strategy to intimidate his assailants or throw them off guard.

Infinity scrambled to grab a fallen log the size of her leg. It was too heavy to be wielded as a nimble weapon, but that was why she'd chosen it. She approached the creature as if she were stupid enough to try to fight him with it.

"What the hell's on this thing?" she heard Hornet say behind her. He was still on the ground—not a good sign. The stone dart must have been poisoned.

The injured creature was pulling the spear from his leg, but he was still on his feet, and soon he'd be able to fight. Things weren't looking good.

"Tourist, this is where you run," she shouted, keeping her eye on the creature and his gyrating hand weapons. She blocked with the log in case he was skilled at throwing either of them. Suddenly, she heard the tourist running, but he wasn't running away. He barreled past her to attack the injured creature with his spear.

The creature facing Infinity saw what was happening, and with an almost-casual flip of his forearm, he threw his stone axe, striking the tourist's head. The tourist collapsed, his body skidding several inches in the dead leaves before coming to a stop. Infinity cursed. There was no time to check on him.

On the bright side, now the creature before her was nothing more than a guy with a knife, which Infinity could handle. As the creature's arm was recovering from throwing the axe, she launched the log, hitting him in the chest. She then kicked him in the nuts and simultaneously double-blocked his knife arm, a combo disarming move she'd practiced a thousand times and had used in more real fights than she cared to remember.

In nine out of ten fights, this move should have flipped the knife harmlessly out of an attacker's hand. But this time it didn't work. The creature was shockingly quick, and he managed to ignore the hit to his groin and counter-block with his free hand, resulting in insufficient leverage on his wrist. He didn't release the knife. In fact, as she disengaged, Infinity felt the stone blade slice her forearm.

Time to switch tactics. The Neanderthal was too skilled with his knife to risk further elaborate moves. She needed to take this fight to the ground, and she needed control of that knife before it killed her. While he was still off-balance from her failed disarming move, she resorted to an animal-like attack on his knife arm. She grabbed his wrist, spun around with her back to him, and tore into his arm with her teeth. This move was another feint, intended to make him think she was desperate and unskilled. Before he could throw his free arm around and transfer the knife to his other hand, she executed her specialty power move, Uchi Mata. She threw her left leg back and up, forcing the man's left leg off the ground. Using his mass against him, she pulled on his arm, hefted him over her shoulders, and slammed him headfirst onto the ground in front of her.

Astoundingly, the creature still hadn't dropped the knife. So instead of trying to break it from his steely grip, she grabbed his knife hand before he could react, bent his arm at the elbow so the knife was above him, and slammed her entire weight onto it. Immediately his muscles began to spasm, indicating he was hurt. She rolled to the side, jumped to her feet, and stepped back to a safe distance.

The creature choked and spat and pulled out the knife, which had been lodged in his throat. It was bloody to the handle, and the wound was definitely mortal. So Infinity turned to face the other Neanderthal, who was still on his feet trying to pull the spear from his meaty thigh. Infinity picked up the tourist's dropped spear and swung it at the man's head, knocking him onto his back. She flipped the spear around and pushed the point into his mouth. The creature gripped the spear, gagging, and stared up at her. But its face wasn't really human, which made her next act all the easier.

"Suck on this, you damn dirty ape." Infinity put all her weight on the spear. She smiled to herself as she watched him die, pleased with her witty quip. She pulled the spear out and wheeled around, scanning the area for other potential threats.

The tourist moaned and rolled to his back. Blood was flowing from his forehead. Infinity stepped over and inspected his head wound. It was a nasty bump, but obviously the axe's blade had not hit him on its sharp edge.

"Just perfect," Infinity grumbled. She walked past the tourist and kneeled beside Hornet. "You going to be okay, partner?"

He was sitting up, holding the stone dart in his hand and staring at it. He turned to her.

"Oh shit," she said. "You don't look so good." This was an understatement. Except for the pupils, his eyes were blood red. His lips were swollen and trembled uncontrollably.

He swallowed loudly. "How much longer, do you think?"

She glanced at the sky, but the trees hid the sun. "It has to be soon."

The tourist got to his feet, swaying as though drunk. "Where's my spear? We've got more company."

Infinity followed the tourist's gaze. He was right. Four more Neanderthal men were standing statue-still at fifty yards, taking in the scene. One of them spoke to the others, and they all smiled.

Infinity put her hand on Hornet's shoulder. "Can you fight right now?"

He struggled to compose himself. Even his lips stopped trembling. "I won't let you down." He grunted and tried to get up.

"Never mind," she said. "You're in no condition to fight."

The creatures let out the same high-pitched scream their fallen companions had. They charged, their atlatls held ready.

Abruptly the Neanderthals were gone, along with everything around them.

─────────────

INFINITY FELL to her knees on the padded floor and retched. But she had done this enough times to keep from purging the meager contents of her gut.

She got to her feet. "The tourist is hurt!" she exclaimed. "Possible concussion or fractured skull. Hornet is hurt, too. Puncture wound to the upper chest or shoulder from a sharpened stone projectile, probably tipped with poison. He's going into shock." She then noticed Hornet was lying facedown on the floor, not moving. "He needs help, now!"

The airlock hatch to the circular, 30-foot bridging chamber opened. Six techs in white biosuits swarmed into the chamber and gathered around the tourist. He was on his knees vomiting, making it difficult to complete their cursory injury assessment.

The tourist finally caught his breath. He turned over and sat on his butt, wiping his mouth. "Can I have some clothes, please?"

Infinity shook her head in disgust. The idiot had thrown all his training out the window as soon as they had bridged thirty-six hours ago. He had refused to follow orders. He'd almost gotten himself killed more than once. She was immensely satisfied knowing he wouldn't be given any clothes for at least three days— only after his patho-cleansing and chemo-cleansing were complete.

Three of the techs helped him to his feet, sat him in a wheelchair, and pushed him to the airlock. As soon as he was able to answer questions, they'd bring him to the post-bridge interview.

Once the tourist was gone, the three remaining techs turned their attention to Hornet.

"His pulse is weak," one of them shouted. "We need a gurney."

After the tourist had cleared the airlock to the next chamber, two more techs came through with a wheeled gurney. It took all five techs to lift Hornet's body onto it. Moments later, Infinity stood alone in the bridging chamber. For the first time, she had the chance to look at the knife wound on her forearm. It was deep. She'd need stitches. It was still bleeding, but not much. No big deal.

"Infinity, do you require medical attention?" The voice had come from a speaker in the ceiling. It was Armando Doyle, Supervisor of Bridgers, Bridge Manager, and CEO of SafeTrek Bridging.

"Maybe a few stitches," she replied. "Worried about Hornet."

"Let the med techs worry about it. You know they're the best. Do you think you can do the post-bridge interview?"

Glaring at Armando through the plexiglass window, she used her right hand to wipe some of the blood from her arm and flung it onto the floor in defiance. "Let's get it over with."

INFINITY and the tourist entered the sealed interview chamber, both of them still naked except for the gel packs that had been quickly taped over their wounds. Everything else could wait. They both could have been infected by parasites that would soon kill them, but as long as they were capable of speaking, the post-bridge interview always came first. This rule was written into SafeTrek's contract with the consortium of universities that had helped fund the facility. They wanted access to information while it was fresh in the minds of bridgers and tourists.

Four men sat on the other side of thick plexiglass, including Armando Doyle. He sat there with his goofy bowtie and gazed at Infinity, like an annoying fatherly figure. She had never seen the others before. The guests were different every time, usually from one university or another. The room used to be full after every excursion, but these days the crowds were sparse. The world was losing interest in bridging. Except for tourists.

Before sitting down, Infinity faced the men. "Go ahead, take a look. After that, focus on me, not my tits."

Armando shook his head at her, but she stood still for several seconds and then sat down behind the barrier designed to conceal only the area below the waist. Like everything else in SafeTrek, the chamber was configured for males.

"You can take a look at me, too," the tourist said, displaying his usual overconfident smile, like everything was a game. Actually, with his wealth everything probably *was* a game. He slowly turned in a circle before sitting down.

The three academics looked a little perturbed, but Armando simply frowned and got straight to business. "We're recording, Infinity. Do you want to start with world specs?"

She nodded. "Forest, plants, and weather pretty much like ours. Surprising, considering a 100,000-year divergence." She was referring to the fact that the tourist had requested a world that had diverged from Earth 100,000 years ago.

Armando turned to the academics. "The client was interested in seeing an alternate path human evolution has taken since their first contact with other hominid species. Although I believe his interest was recreational rather than academic."

The men nodded with furrowed brows, as if they considered a recreational excursion to be a waste of time.

"I'm sitting right here," the tourist said. "I can speak for myself. It turns out 100,000 years was a good choice on my part. I saw exactly what I was hoping for. In that timeline, Neanderthals probably wiped out humans—Neanderthals were all we saw."

"We saw at least six," Infinity said. "All were nonhuman. Maybe Neanderthal. Maybe some other species. We only covered a few miles, so we don't know if humans also existed on the same world." She knew at least one of the academics would want a full description of the creatures, so she described them in detail.

"These things were badass," the tourist said before she could finish her recounting. "I think they were out hunting for pleasure, like when we go big game hunting. Only these guys used handheld weapons, like it was a matter of pride to them. The minute they spotted us, they started hunting us." He smiled and shook his head. "They were badass."

Infinity rolled her eyes. This guy never quit. The academics would want details on the Neanderthals' weapons, so she described them.

"Can you describe any of the plants you saw?" one of the men asked. "Particularly any that were unusual?"

"I don't know much about plants," Infinity replied. "To me they looked like the plants outside this building." Then she sighed. "Maybe you should bridge somewhere yourself."

Armando frowned at her. "A little respect, Infinity."

She shrugged and nodded. She was the best bridger at Safe-Trek, so Armando usually cut her some slack. Still, she would be nothing if he hadn't hired her. If he wanted her to behave, she would at least try.

"I saw some birds," she offered. "I'd never seen birds with feather markings like these had, but their basic shapes weren't much different. Saw some squirrels. At least three wild cats smaller than bobcats. No deer or anything like that. Perhaps Neanderthal hunters killed all those."

This was followed by a stream of questions about details, like the smell of the air, the color of the sky, the weight of the Neanderthals, their language, their clothing, and any signs of disease or malformations. She answered the questions the best she could. Lucky for her, the tourist had finally shut up. Probably bored.

The academics listened attentively to every word. And they frantically scribbled notes, even though they knew they'd get a copy of the interview video.

The questions were finally beginning to slow down when Armando held a finger up so he could listen to someone talking to him in his earpiece. He frowned and shook his head. "Thank you, Celia," he said. He looked through the glass at Infinity. "I'm sorry to tell you this. Hornet didn't make it. The techs think you may have been correct. Poison on the stone dart."

Infinity stared down at her hands in her lap. The tourist next to her was talking. Something about Hornet being a badass, too. She shot up from her chair and glared at him. For just a moment she considered pummeling the idiot. But bridgers didn't harm tourists. Ever. Instead, she slammed her fist into the plexiglass. She hit it again, hard enough that the gel pack on her forearm flew off and her blood splattered the clear barrier.

The academics drew back, eyes wide.

Armando stood up. "Gentlemen, we'll end the interview here if you don't mind." He then motioned them to the door.

The tourist said, "Can I go now, too? I have a splitting headache."

Armando nodded, and a tech came through the hatch and escorted the tourist out.

Armando turned to Infinity once they were alone. "Are you finished, kiddo?"

"Don't call me that. Not right now."

"I'm sorry." He sat silently for a moment, tugging on his bowtie with two fingers. "And I'm sorry about Hornet. He was a good bridger. Maybe the best."

She studied his face. When she saw the slight grin, she relaxed a little. "Good, but not the best," she muttered. He was only trying to cheer her up.

His smile broadened. It was genuine, not forced. "His salary will go to his beneficiary for five years. That's the deal."

She just shook her head. Like her, Hornet had no family to speak of. He had never told her who he'd chosen as his beneficiary. He'd been a drifter before signing up at SafeTrek, so probably some kid somewhere who didn't even know he had a father.

"Well, after your cleansings, take three days bereavement. Or whatever it is you like to do when you lose a partner. Then I need you back here. We have a rather unusual excursion coming up. I want my best bridgers involved."

Infinity eyed him warily. "Coming up when?"

"Could be as soon as August third."

"That's three weeks. How in the hell am I supposed to—"

He held up a hand. "You'll be paid double for the upcoming excursion. Plus, you won't be docked for bringing your tourist back tonight with eight qualifying wounds to his body and possibly a concussion."

Now she looked at him with outright suspicion. "What are you getting me into?"

"Like I said, it's a rather unusual excursion. The clients will arrive August first. You'll train them on the second. If our first bio-probe is successful, the bridge could take place August third. But they've blocked out the entire month in case it requires multiple bio-probes."

Infinity slapped her palm on the plexiglass, smearing her own blood. "Two things about what you just said are screwed up. What do you mean, *clients*? I'm not taking two tourists again." It was always difficult babysitting one tourist. She had taken two before. It was too risky, too damn chaotic.

"No, you're not," he said. "You're taking three."

She pressed harder against the plexiglass and the seams began to creak under the pressure. "You're not serious."

Armando glanced at the seams but refused to show concern. He nodded. "They've got the money. In fact, they've pre-paid. They're going, Infinity, and you're taking them. You and the bridger you choose for your new partner. Next question."

She closed her eyes and tried to slow her breathing. She was almost afraid to ask her next question. Tourists got to choose how far back the point of divergence would be. If the destination world had diverged from ours five minutes ago, it would be virtually iden-tical. If it had diverged a year ago, there might be noticeable differ-ences. A lot can happen in a year. With a divergence 1,000 years ago, civilization could look quite different. At 100,000 years, humans may not even exist, as with this latest fiasco. Neanderthals or some other species could have gotten the upper hand at some point. Infinity hated bridging to worlds that had diverged much beyond 1,000 years ago. Things got too unpredictable. She could fight any human alive, because she understood how humans fought. But as she had been reminded today, it was hard to know how a nonhuman would fight.

She opened her eyes slowly. "And why do you think the first bio-probe won't be successful? How far back do they want the divergence?" The bio-probe was how SafeTrek found an inhabit-able world, one that didn't have toxic air, lethal temperatures, or some other instant-death deal-breaker. Worlds with divergence in the distant past were much more likely to be uninhabitable due to all the possible environmental changes that could have occurred during that time.

Armando forced a smile. "You might want to sit down first, kiddo."

She pushed even harder on the clear barrier. "Just spit it out."

"The clients were very specific in their request, and they were willing to pay all additional fees." He hesitated. "You'll be escorting them to a world that diverged from ours eighty million years ago."

2

TREMORS

August 2 — Seventeen days later

DESMOND WEAVER FELT the ground shaking, which broke his concentration. He lowered his guard for a moment, and the four-foot dinosaur maneuvered around his crude, two-pronged spear and went straight for his throat.

"You're dead, Weaver. Again." The trainer known as Razor shoved the pole with its attached dinosaur, smacking Desmond in the face with the ridiculous rubber creature.

"I felt another tremor," Desmond said. "It distracted me."

Desmond's college roommate, Xavier Cahill, looked at his watch. "That's three tremors in the last hour." Xavier was the only guy Desmond knew who actually wore a watch. He and Desmond's other roommate, Lenny Stiles, were standing on the sidelines waiting for their turn to battle the fake dinosaur with their own hand-made spears.

Lenny said, "I'm telling you guys, we're at the cusp of a zip-banging bitch of an apocalypse. Mark my words." Lenny had been saying that for a year, since the quakes and unusual weather had started.

"Again," Razor said, and he held the dinosaur out, ready to attack.

Desmond sighed and raised his spear. The two-pronged spears would be the first weapons they'd make after bridging to their destination world, assuming there were any plants with suitable stems. Razor had explained that spears were the easiest weapons to make with their bare hands. Anything shorter than a spear was pretty much useless against animal attacks. He had demonstrated that almost any predator could be held at bay with a long spear, even if the creature had a five-foot reach with its teeth or claws.

Desmond sparred with the dinosaur again. This time he managed to puncture it with one of the sharpened tips, but this only triggered Razor to animate the creature more vigorously, as if it had become enraged. Seconds later, Desmond received another embarrassing smack to the face.

Razor grunted, "You're dead, Weaver. Again." The guy wasn't prone to long speeches. He often spoke in one-word sentences. Razor was a completely hairless, lean fighting machine. According to the SafeTrek website, for twenty years he had trained U.S. Army soldiers in hand-to-hand combat. And since the start of their training early that morning, he had made Desmond, Lenny, and Xavier realize, beyond any doubt, that they knew basically nothing about defending themselves. But to his credit, he had taught them two things: first, tourists had to allow their bridgers—in this case Razor and his partner Infinity—to protect them if there was any kind of attack. And second, they learned a few basic skills to help them stay alive if both bridgers were killed.

"Again," Razor said.

Desmond jammed the butt of his spear into the grass at his feet and held it vertically. "Razor, I see what you're trying to do. But training for a few hours isn't going to make us effective fighters. It's a safe bet there won't be humans on our destination world. And honestly, I'm betting there won't be dinosaurs either. The chances are slim."

Razor shook the rubber Dinosaur. "You know what predators will be there?"

"That's the whole idea," Desmond said. "There's no way to predict which megafauna will have become dominant in a complete do-over of the last eighty million years."

"Exactly." He shook the dinosaur again. "Defend yourself."

Xavier got to his feet and stepped forward. "Desmond is right. It would be a better use of our time if *we* were to train *you* to help us make the observations he needs for his dissertation. If we're attacked by predators, you guys will protect us. That's your job, isn't it?"

"Don't answer that, Razor!"

The demand came from Razor's partner. Other than having briefly introduced herself after breakfast, this was the first time she had spoken. For the last three hours she had been sitting atop a boulder at the side of the training field behind the SafeTrek building, silently watching the training exercises. Desmond had finally decided she must have been meditating.

She unfolded her legs, got to her feet, and jumped to the ground. She landed lightly and approached the group. She wore nothing more than a tight-fitting sports top and shorts, like a mixed martial arts fighter. Which was exactly what she had been before joining SafeTrek. Unlike Razor's smooth scalp, her head had a few weeks of hair growth. A fresh, brightly-colored tattoo of a bird covered most of her chest, in contrast with the smaller, faded Safe-Trek tattoo on her arm. Scars of various sizes and stages of healing adorned the rest of her body, including a recently-stitched three-inch slice on her right forearm. To Desmond, she was intimidating, but she was also beautiful in her own scary, look-at-me-wrong-and-I'll-slit-your-throat kind of way. Her name was Infinity Fowler.

She stopped in front of Desmond and Xavier. Lenny was still sitting, and she snapped her fingers at him and then pointed at a spot on the ground next to Desmond. Lenny quickly got up and stepped to the spot. Razor stood to the side with his arms crossed.

Finally, she spoke. "When we're together, who's God?"

After several seconds of silence, Desmond looked at Xavier and then at Lenny. They just shrugged, offering no help.

He turned back to Infinity. "You are?"

"Wrong. You are." She glanced at Lenny and Xavier. "And you, and you. Why? Because I'd die to save your life. How about you, Razor?"

"Damn right I would," he said.

She stepped closer to Desmond. Uncomfortably close. "We're bridgers. We'd die to save you from a flesh wound, tourist. How does that make you feel?"

Again there was silence.

"I guess I feel lucky," Desmond said. "And safe." He then tried to hold her intense gaze without looking away.

She broke eye contact first. Her eyes moved down to his t-shirt, and then to his khaki shorts, and finally to his water sandals before moving back to his face. "You don't think our exercises are very real."

"I didn't say that. It's just that—"

"You're right."

Desmond wasn't sure how to respond. He just shook his head.

"So far it's not real," she said.

Razor nodded. "Let's make it real."

Suddenly they both peeled off their tight shorts, and then Infinity pulled her sports top off over her head. They stood buck naked, staring at Desmond, Xavier, and Lenny.

The silence reached a new level of uncomfortable.

"Bridging strips away nonliving matter," Infinity said. "You come out the other side like you came out of your mama—naked, bald, and scared. For most tourists we don't get real until after lunch. But you're ready. Shed your clothes."

Lenny smiled and said, "I figured this was coming. I got no problem with it." He started stripping.

Desmond sighed. They'd all be naked together for the thirty-six hours of the excursion. Might as well get used to it now. He flipped his sandals off.

"I'd like to request to leave my underwear on," Xavier said. "I see no reason to go this far before bridging."

Desmond had been Xavier's roommate long enough to suspect something like this might happen. He frowned at Xavier and then turned to Infinity to see how she would handle it.

She was eyeing him back. "You in charge?"

Desmond shrugged as he removed his shorts. "Xavier's paying for the whole thing."

"Who talked who into it?"

He forced a half grin as he removed his underwear. "That would be me. I'm doing this for my dissertation. I need their help with observations."

She nodded. "Then you're in charge. You've got a problem. You have one minute to fix it." She then stepped over to Razor and they began talking softly.

Desmond turned again to Xavier and Lenny. "I had no intention of being in charge."

Lenny was naked now. He held up both hands. "It's all zippity-doo-dah with me, Des. You can be in charge."

Xavier was frowning. "I don't care who's in charge. But I'm not comfortable removing my underwear until we absolutely have to. Especially in front of her." He tilted his head toward Infinity.

Desmond shot a glance at the bridgers. She had said *one minute*. What would she do if this took longer? He turned back to his friends. "Okay, here's the way I see it. This is costing half a million apiece. That's one-point-five million dollars. It's your family's money, Xavier. You want to waste it all by screwing this up?"

Gazing at Xavier, Lenny nodded. "It'd be wicked-crisp if you'd just shed your damn shorts, man."

Xavier mumbled something and started taking them off. "Why do you have to talk that way? What does *wicked-crisp* even mean? You just made it up."

Lenny smiled. "Wicked-crisp, man. It means everything you aren't. There's stuff that is wicked-crisp, and then there's you."

Desmond ignored their banter and turned back to the bridgers, involuntarily putting one hand over his groin. He called out, "Problem solved."

Infinity walked over and faced him again. "Like I said, you're in charge." She reached behind Desmond's head and pulled the end of his ponytail around to the front. "How long did it take you to grow this?"

"I don't know. Couple years."

She stroked the hair like it was a pet. "Too bad." She looked him in the eye. "Desmond's a pussy name. We'll call you Decay."

She turned to Lenny. "Lenny's a pussy name, too. We'll call you Lynch."

Lenny smiled like a teenager. "I can live with that."

"What'll you call me?" Xavier asked.

She shot him a quick glance. "Xavier suits you fine."

Desmond said, "If you don't mind, I'll keep my own name. And Lenny will, too. It'll facilitate communication."

Infinity raised her brows, although they were merely stubble, still growing back from her last bridge. "Earn them back by the end of the day. Starting now, things are gonna be real. This way."

She and Razor then walked off the manicured lawn of the Safe-Trek training field and into the sweltering, bug-infested Missouri forest.

AN HOUR later they were still walking. Desmond was trying to guess how far they'd come when he felt the ground tremble again. He needed to inspect his feet for thorns, so he spoke to the bridgers, hoping they'd stop to answer his question. "What do you guys think about all the recent earthquakes?"

Infinity and Razor paused and frowned at each other. "You're the scientists," Infinity said.

Desmond noticed his left foot was bleeding, and his legs had been scratched by weeds from the knees down. He also had a few cuts on his arms and a few dozen mosquito bites. Xavier and Lenny stopped just behind him and began checking their own bodies.

"We're all biologists, not geologists," Xavier said. "But I've read speculation that rising ocean levels from global warming are affecting the tectonic plates in some ways no one had predicted."

"We're screwing ourselves big-time," Lenny added.

Desmond said, "I just thought since you guys are bridgers, you've seen things no one else has seen. Alternate versions of Earth. I thought maybe you'd have a different perspective."

Razor simply shook his head.

Infinity said, "Some idiots blame the bridging centers."

Desmond was glad she hadn't forced him to bring this up. There were seven bridging centers around the globe, and since the first one had been created four years ago, conspiracy theorists had come up with all manner of doomsday scenarios. And when the weather events and tremors had started, they had all gone into paranoia overdrive. "Yeah, but as far as I know they don't have any evidence to support the notion. I was going to ask your thoughts on it."

She shrugged. "I'm just a bridger."

The bridgers turned and continued leading them to some unknown destination.

"Where exactly are we going?" Xavier called out.

"We're walking," Razor replied.

"But *where* are we walking? My feet are bleeding."

Infinity grabbed Razor's elbow and the two bridgers stopped. She said, "Good. Maybe you deserve a non-pussy name after all. But it shouldn't take you so long to ask the right questions. Now that you ask, we're not walking anywhere. We're just walking. And now that you're aware of how to do it wrong, it's time to learn how to do it right."

Razor pointed at the ground. "Every step, choose where you put your feet. Avoid rocks, they can cut you and they can be slippery. Avoid sticks, they can break and reveal your presence. Avoid brush, the stems can scratch, and the leaves can inject painful histamines, like stinging nettles. Or they can secrete rash-inducing compounds, like poison ivy. When you're naked, everything can be a threat. Be aware of your surroundings, no matter how insignificant things seem."

This was the most Razor had said at one time.

Xavier said, "You mean we walked all this way because you were waiting for someone to ask where we're going?"

"Walking naked in a harsh environment is real training," Razor said. "After we bridge, that's what you'll be doing. Now we're going to walk back, and you're not going to have one additional scratch when we get there."

Lenny laughed. "I love these bridgers, Des—I mean Decay. They're the real deal." He turned to Razor and Infinity. "I'm one-hundred percent on board. Lead the way."

"You don't get it, Lynch," Infinity said. "You're leading the way back."

WHEN THEY FINALLY EMERGED FROM the trees onto the training

field, the sun had dropped behind the forest canopy. Desmond was drenched in sweat. But he had to admit the experience had made him more confident. He now knew he could move through a wild environment while naked without killing himself in the process. They had learned to negotiate deep ravines without cutting their feet, climb trees without scraping their skin off on the bark, and pass through thick and thorny brush without losing an eye. They had even practiced sitting perfectly still, not moving a muscle or even blinking, which Razor had said was the most effective way to avoid predators.

A large pan of pasta with white sauce was waiting for them on a picnic table, kept warm atop an electric heating coil. The idea was to load up on carbs, since they might bridge as early as tomorrow morning. It was likely they wouldn't eat anything during the thirty-six-hour excursion.

They heaped food onto plates and sat at the picnic table beneath the looming block-like SafeTrek building. Their clothes were neatly folded at one end of the table, but now they were beyond caring about being naked, and no one bothered to expend the energy needed to get up and put them on. They ate in silence until they had all finished the food on their first plates and loaded them up a second time.

"Have we earned our real names back yet?" Desmond asked.

Infinity scooped some pasta into her mouth. She shrugged. Then she nodded.

"Thanks," he said awkwardly. "Speaking of names, what's up with Infinity? And Razor? Those aren't your real names, are they?"

"They are to you, tourist," Razor said.

Xavier spoke while stirring his pasta around on his plate with his fork. "So that's how it's going to be, even after we almost killed ourselves trying to make you guys happy?"

"It's a bridger thing," Infinity said. "We take on new names when we come aboard. Like becoming a Ramone."

Lenny dropped his fork. "Zippity-what? The Ramones? Infinity, are you trying to make me fall in love?"

Infinity and Razor turned to Lenny with glares that made Desmond worry Lenny was about to get punched in the face.

Lenny picked up his fork. "Sorry. I was just...." He went back to eating.

"What are the names of the other bridgers here?" Xavier asked.

Infinity spoke around a mouthful of food. "Seven bridgers at SafeTrek. Three partner pairs and one backup. Others are Wraith, Trencher, Viper, Falcon, and Fang."

"That's awesome," Lenny said. He seemed to have recovered from the embarrassment of his tactless faux pas.

Desmond wasn't sure he wanted to know the answer to his next question, but he asked anyway. "Why is there a backup bridger?"

Infinity and Razor exchanged a glance. "Bridgers do excursions in pairs," she said. "If we lose a partner, we get a new one."

Desmond wondered how often this happened, but the way the bridgers suddenly looked down at their plates made him think better of asking.

Xavier shoved his empty plate to the center of the table. "So, what can we expect for tonight?"

"What time is it?" Infinity asked.

Xavier looked at his watch, which he hadn't removed when he had stripped down. "Just after 6:30."

Razor and Infinity both took one more bite and then stood up.

"Time to go," Infinity said. "Put your clothes on. They want you there for the bio-probe results."

———

THE BRIDGERS LED them back into the SafeTrek building and through several long corridors to a small, empty room. One wall consisted of a thick plexiglass window into the next room, which was larger but also empty.

Soon after, they were joined by Armando Doyle, who was apparently the bridgers' boss. He was also the man who had happily accepted their million and a half dollars. As he stepped into the room, he made a comical gesture of grabbing his bow tie with both hands and rocking it back and forth. He then maneuvered awkwardly around Infinity and Razor to get to the tourists to shake their hands vigorously.

"I trust your orientation day has been adequately productive." He looked them up and down. "You certainly look less haggard than most of our clients at this stage of the game. Well done. Well done indeed. We're all quite proud of Infinity and Razor. You're fortunate to have them on your team."

The two bridgers stared at Doyle as he spoke. They didn't nod or smile.

"I think we all feel ready for our excursion," Desmond said.

Doyle glanced at the smartwatch on his wrist. "Right, on to business. At precisely 3.6 seconds after 7:00 PM, we will learn the results of our first bio-probe. Often a first bio-probe will be successful, and I'm optimistic yours will be as well. But due to your rather unusual excursion specifications—specifically an eighty-million-year divergence—success is not guaranteed. If the bio-probe is unsuccessful, we will begin a second bio-probe tomorrow at 7:00 AM, with the results coming thirty-six hours after that, at 7:00 PM the following evening. And so on, until we have a successful probe."

"Something I've been wondering about," said Xavier. "Why are bio-probes and excursions always thirty-six hours? Why not make them twenty-four hours, or forty-eight?"

Doyle smiled and nodded. "Of course, all will be explained. But certain details of our operations will only be revealed after we have a successful bio-probe, indicating a safe destination world, upon which you will sign our non-disclosure agreement. Provided, of course, that you still plan to proceed with the excursion."

Xavier huffed out a laugh. "Considering you only refund half the cost, I don't think we're going to change our minds."

Doyle smiled broadly. "People never do." He looked at his watch again. "Almost time. A bit of explanation is in order. Our bio-probe is quite simple. As I'm sure you know, nonliving objects and matter do not make it through a bridge. So we can't send probes or other measuring devices. Our only choice is to send a diverse set of living mammals to the destination world. Thirty-six hours later, when they return, we analyze their condition. If they are intact and reasonably healthy, we then allow you, our clients, to make the final decision as to whether you want to bridge to the same location. This is why you are here in this room. We want you to see the returning test animals yourself, so that you may be confident and well-informed in your decision."

Doyle pointed through the clear barrier. "The test animals will appear at the vertical and horizontal center of the chamber. They will be a few inches apart from each other, regardless of their spatial arrangement in the alternate world. They will fall to the padded floor, and then our techs—wearing protective suits—will immediately enter the chamber to evaluate their condition. Our standard set of test mammals includes two Dorset sheep, two Florida white rabbits, two domestic cats, two guinea pigs, two rats, and two mice." He glanced at his watch yet again. "Less than a minute. Any questions?"

Desmond had a million questions but decided to wait and see what would happen.

They arranged themselves so that everyone had a clear view into the chamber and then waited. Desmond could feel his heart beating as the seconds passed.

"Watch carefully," Doyle said.

The air in the larger room wavered visibly, and then the plexiglass window flexed outward toward the observers, as if the pressure had suddenly increased in the chamber. A group of shapes appeared and abruptly dropped to the floor. Some of them floundered for a moment and began running around the room, obviously terrified. Others didn't move at all. A few of them, in fact, appeared to be nothing but piles of dark goo. All of them were totally devoid of hair.

Doyle clapped his hands together. "Astounding—the first bio-probe is a success!"

A hatch to the chamber opened, and white-suited technicians swarmed in and began rounding up the creatures. Working in pairs, one held an animal still while the other took readings with skin-surface thermometers and miscellaneous other probes. Two technicians moved directly to the center of the room to evaluate the animals that weren't moving. This included one of the sheep, its pink-skinned body apparently having been partially eaten.

Doyle spoke excitedly. "Considering the extreme divergence time you requested, I am mildly surprised we were able to find a habitable world on the first try. The number of factors that could have acted upon the planet's geology and biosphere is astronomical. For example, a new type of plant could have evolved more efficient food production that doesn't create oxygen as a byproduct, outcompeting the flowering plants and rendering the atmosphere toxic to us. Random climatic events could have occurred, changing ocean temperatures so that the entire central United States is still submerged under a shallow sea. The possibilities are nearly endless."

Infinity sighed loudly. "Half the animals are dead. One sheep is partially eaten. A predator large enough to—"

"Yes, yes, Infinity. That appears to be the case. I'm simply expressing my surprise at the bio-probe's success."

Doyle's enthusiasm was contagious, and Desmond wasn't keen on two more days of training with Infinity and Razor while waiting for the next bio-probe. He said, "The sheep didn't have two bridgers there to protect them."

"Yes, precisely," Doyle said. "Let's see what the techs have to tell us, shall we?"

They moved to a small conference room and sat around a glass-top table. They made mostly-awkward small talk for about ten minutes. Finally, a woman in her thirties wearing shorts and a long-sleeve denim shirt came in, took a seat at the table, and silently studied a tablet she had brought with her.

"This is Celia Pickett," Doyle said. "She has a knack for comprehensively summarizing bio-probe results, allowing for prompt bridging decisions."

The woman glanced up from her tablet for a split second. She wore dangly earrings and closely cropped black hair—no more than a centimeter in length. Perhaps she had bridged recently. Or maybe she was showing solidarity with the bridgers.

Everyone waited silently.

Finally, the woman looked up. "The bio-probe specimens returning alive showed no signs of extreme temperatures, elevated radiation levels, or low blood oxygen. Minimal dehydration." She glanced at Desmond, Lenny, and Xavier. "Micro or macro parasites picked up on an excursion are not bridged back. But it is often possible to detect their recent presence on or in the body—surface scarring, telltale changes in blood chemistry, that sort of thing. The bio-probe animals showed signs of ecto-parasites, or perhaps biting insects, but probably no more than what the three of you experienced during your training exercises today."

Lenny held up his hand like he was in a classroom. "What about stomach contents? If the animals eat while they're there, can you see what they've eaten?"

She smiled and nodded, as if to say this was a good question. "Foreign matter doesn't bridge back to our world, even if it's inside the body, except for basic components that have already been broken down and have entered the body's cells. Whatever bridged out, bridges back. No more, no less. Particularly if the test specimen is still alive."

Lenny seemed to consider this. "So if one of the animals dies on the other world—what exactly happens?"

"It depends on the condition of the tissue. To put it simply, the more intact the tissue is, the more likely it will bridge back to our world. This is a result of the specific tagging process we use to prepare you for bridging." She shot a glance at Doyle. "I can tell you more of the technicals after your official briefing."

Xavier smirked. "You mean after we sign a non-disclosure agreement."

She smiled but didn't confirm it. "The biggest concern now is the mortality rate of the bio-probe animals. Of the twelve test animals, five returned dead or did not return at all. Which means not only are they dead, but their cells are no longer intact."

Desmond leaned forward over the table. "What would cause their cells to no longer be intact after only thirty-six hours?"

"Incineration for one. But, much more likely, chemical breakdown—digestion."

After a few seconds, Lenny said, "Daaamn...."

Celia switched off her tablet. "Unfortunately, that's the extent of what we can learn from a bio-probe."

"Thank you, Celia," Doyle said. He then turned to Infinity and Razor. "Your thoughts for our clients?"

The bridgers had been silent throughout the discussion.

Infinity cleared her throat. "Five of twelve dead. I don't like it."

Doyle gazed at her. "And?"

"And that's my input. The world's predator-heavy. I don't like it."

Razor shrugged. "It's not ideal. But I've bridged after worse than five of twelve. I could go either way—fifty-fifty."

Doyle raised his brows at the bridgers, but apparently they had no intention of saying more. He turned to Desmond, Lenny, and Xavier at the opposite end of the table. "In situations like this, our clients make the final decision. If you accept this world, you'll bridge at 7:00 AM tomorrow. If you decline, we'll initiate another bio-probe."

Desmond looked at his friends.

Lenny smiled broadly. "I'm here for the ride, Des," he said, nodding to Infinity and Razor. "With these two bridgers, we'll put some zippity-smackdown on this predator-heavy world. Let's get it done."

Xavier furrowed his brows and shook his head at Lenny's response. "Since this is an *important* decision, I'll give a more mature, measured opinion. Do I like the idea of a 'predator-heavy' world?" He made quotation marks in the air. "No. But I do like the idea of proceeding immediately. I was prepared to be here for as long as it takes, but, to be honest, the idea of completing this excursion and still having a few weeks of summer before the semester— well, that's rather intoxicating. I vote we do it."

Lenny huffed. "That's pretty much what I just said, man."

Desmond glanced at Infinity. She was staring at him with a face of stone. He then turned to Doyle. "I guess we're bridging in the morning."

3

BRIEFING

August 2 — 30 minutes later

EYES HALF CLOSED, Infinity forced from her mind the flood of visual scenarios and well-practiced techniques for killing things both human and nonhuman. Clearing her mind was no easy task— she would bridge in less than twelve hours. When practicing the silent meditative state known as Mokuso, it was essential to clear away images of violence. Which was why she wasn't all that good at Mokuso.

She stared at the floor in front of her to minimize distractions. Inhaling through her nose, she visualized the air moving up through her forehead, across the crown of her skull, and down her spine, finally collecting in her lower abdomen, winding in ever-shrinking circles until it disappeared into a tiny point. She exhaled slowly and repeated the process until her mind was at peace.

Several minutes later the alarm next to her bed broke her trance. She sighed, got up from the floor, and turned it off.

Infinity considered every minute of life to be sacred. Driving back and forth from SafeTrek to an apartment elsewhere would mean wasted minutes. So she had insisted on her own permanent bunkroom in the SafeTrek building. Armando had agreed to this, although he had reminded her more than once that she might have more of a social life if she'd live off-site. Armando tended to treat her like a daughter sometimes. Considering Infinity hadn't seen her real father since she was fourteen, she didn't usually mind.

She stepped over to her sink, wiped her eyes with her palms, and looked in the mirror. She saw the face of a killer. The truth of this bothered her more every year. But it was the truth nevertheless. A few more years and she'd have enough money saved to quit bridging and do something normal—something that had nothing to do with fighting or killing.

"You afraid?" She asked aloud. The face in the mirror looked calm and relaxed, which wasn't at all how she felt. "You'd better be," she said, finally.

She ran her fingers over her scalp and its seventeen-day growth. She could still see the dark scar she'd gotten from a broken bottle when she was fifteen. Two more weeks and her hair would've been long enough to hide it. Only once in the last year had her hair grown out that long.

She looked at the clock and sighed. Turning back to the mirror, she said, "And you'd better be able to sleep tonight."

She rubbed cold water on her face, dried it off, and left her room.

INFINITY WAS the last to sit down at the briefing table. By now the tourists had likely spent the last ten minutes signing non-disclosure agreements and bitching about this clause or that clause. The forms were stupidly long and confusing. But Infinity could summarize them in one sentence: keep your damn mouth shut about everything except what you see and do between bridge-out and bridge-back.

Briefings were limited to just a few people. Armando and Celia were there to provide information, the tourists were supposed to listen and ask questions, and the two bridgers would answer questions they were allowed to answer. Infinity was always bored by the briefings—she had heard it all before. But she did like to watch the tourists' reactions to what they learned. You could learn a lot about someone through those reactions. And the more she knew, the better she could get them to cooperate when excursions went south.

Once Infinity sat down, Armando nodded to Celia, and she didn't waste time. Which was something Infinity always appreciated.

"This may seem like an unusual topic to begin the briefing with," Celia said to the tourists, "but it is important to provide you with some background. Again, I'll remind you of your non-disclosure obligations. Leaking this information will not only result in federal charges against you, but it will also automatically triple your financial obligation to SafeTrek." She paused and waited until the tourists nodded.

"As I'm sure you know, five years ago, humans experienced a significant turning point for science, as well as theology, anthropology, and sociology." She touched her tablet, which activated a projector, displaying on the wall a photo of the now-famous ATA—the Allen Telescope Array—in the Cascade Mountains of California.

The three tourists exchanged confused glances. They had no idea what was coming.

Celia went on. "The Allen Telescope Array detected a repeating set of non-natural radio waves transmitted simultaneously at numerous frequencies between 1,420 and 1,720 megahertz, proving beyond any doubt that at least one intelligent civilization exists besides our own. The extraterrestrials were

dubbed in popular culture as the Outlanders, as the signal origi-
nated farther from the center of the galactic plane than Earth."

The motormouth tourist—Xavier—started to say something but
then stopped and waited.

"The transmitted signals had finally been decoded several
months after their discovery. The general public knows that the
signals included information about the aliens and their civilization,
like a more robust version of the golden records we sent out of our
solar system on the Voyagers 1 and 2, or the crude plaques sent
onboard Pioneers 10 and 11."

Finally the motormouth couldn't help himself. "May I ask what
this has to do with our excursion?"

Celia nodded. "There are other segments of the Outlanders'
signal the general public does not know about."

The tourists exchanged another look, this time with a touch of
holy-shit on their faces. The next few minutes would be the most
amusing part of Infinity's day.

"An international committee representing the governments of
twenty-one countries decided some segments of the information
were to be withheld and used judiciously. Primarily, detailed
instructions for creating a bridging device."

All three tourists sat up straight and stared, apparently too
shocked to speak.

Now the briefing was getting real. Infinity watched the tourists
carefully.

Celia continued. "Contrary to what you've heard in the media,
bridging technology is far beyond human science. Before we built
the bridging centers, many physicists didn't even believe that there
were infinite parallel universes. We only had a basic theoretical
notion of the concept, and were hundreds of years—maybe thousands—from developing a way to transport living things between
realities. To put it bluntly, we have no idea how the bridging
devices work."

Still the tourists stared silently, trying to process what they'd heard. When they finally regained the ability to speak, they displayed the same sequence of reactions Infinity had seen so many times before: denial, outrage, and then numerous questions. The motormouth Xavier was considering pulling out of the deal. But now that the final agreement forms had been signed, there would be no refund. So now he was pouting like a kid. The agreeable Lenny, on the other hand, had already decided this knowledge would only enhance the adventure. And the leader, Desmond—he was the one who'd make or break the whole excursion. Now he was silently considering things. Infinity wasn't sure what to think of Desmond. He typically kept his mouth shut unless he had something worthwhile to say. Infinity could identify with that trait. But when Desmond did speak, his buddies listened. If things got rough on the excursion, she'd have to focus on getting Desmond in line first. She found herself wondering what he'd look like after bridging took his hair, but she quickly pushed the thought from her mind.

For the next half-hour, Celia went through the rest of the most critical information, occasionally projecting photos and graphics on the screen. The bridging device allowed you to dial back accurately to whatever divergence point you wanted, but no one understood how. For each possible divergence point, there were seemingly infinite worlds available, but one world was selected randomly by the device. Once you initially accessed a specific world, the window to that particular universe remained available for only about 108 hours, after which the connection was severed and you could never find that world again. No one knew why bridging stripped away hair, clothing, dead skin cells, and other nonliving matter. Nor did anyone know where these things disappeared to. Bridging back was made possible by a scanning and tagging procedure performed before bridging out. Each excursion lasted slightly over thirty-six hours. This was due to the half-life of the tagging radioisotope, but no one knew why that particular isotope was the only one that worked.

Finally, Celia tapped her tablet, and the projector went dark. She was finished.

Armando Doyle groaned softly as he stood up. "And that, gentlemen, is why you signed a non-disclosure agreement. If it were up to me, I'd make this information available to everyone. But the powers that be, in their infinite wisdom, have decided that the general public does not need to know that bridging technology came from the Outlanders. I suppose I can see their point. Folks would argue that any information from a distant civilization should be freely available to all citizens of Earth. And it's conceivable they would win that argument in court." He raised his hands like a preacher. "But can you imagine if everyone with the resources had the ability to create bridging devices?"

"Bridging would be less expensive," Xavier said.

Armando smiled. "Perhaps. But there must be order. Would you want bridging centers catering to people who desire to bridge to parallel worlds so that they could commit murder or rape? Or to people who fantasize about wiping out an entire city? Or worse? Oh yes, there are people who have requested such excursions from us. But we strive to keep a measure of order."

He started pacing around the table. "And the truth of the matter is that bridging is dangerous. That's why we have highly-qualified bridgers like Infinity and Razor. As the three of you obviously know, bridging to alternate worlds could be one of the richest sources of scientific data imaginable. Scientists, not to mention experts in a thousand other fields, should be lining up at our doors, booking their data-collecting excursions years in advance. But they're not. Do you know why?"

Desmond spoke up. "Because none of that data can be brought back. It's limited to what researchers can fit into their own minds and recall when they return."

"Precisely," Armando said. "And beyond that—"

"And that's why I'm here," Desmond said, cutting him off. "I have an advantage over most other researchers."

Armando raised his brows.

"I have an elevated capacity to remember certain things," Desmond said. "Some people call it a photographic memory, but that's an oversimplification."

Infinity leaned forward in her chair. There might be more to this Desmond than she had thought.

"Given the right kind of observations," he said, "I can recall thousands of chunks of information. You said you will be providing us with recording devices as soon as we return, and I plan to do a serious info-dump. All of which I can then analyze later for my dissertation. That's why I requested that no other researchers be present at the post-bridge interview—intellectual property and all that."

"That is quite fascinating," Armando said. "If only there were more minds like yours. I'm afraid bridging by researchers has declined in the four years since our facility opened. We have compensated for this by offering excursions as a form of recreation. But the, um, physical hardships of the bridging process are a deterrent to all but the most determined adventure-seekers, some of whom we must refuse due to their interest in non-allowable activities. We've been forced to increase our prices significantly to remain viable."

"I have a question," the motormouth said. "Why do you think the Outlanders included instructions for constructing bridging devices in their radio signals?"

Armando put a finger to his chin like he was thinking about this for the first time. But Infinity knew he had been puzzling over it for years.

"Perhaps it was their greatest achievement, and they were simply proud," he said. "I like to think it was because there is some-

thing much more useful about bridging, something that was so intu-
itive to them that they didn't bother to mention it. Perhaps it's
something we will eventually discover on our own."

Infinity was getting bored and decided it was time to speak up.
"Are we on for the morning or off? I've got prepping to do."

"As do I," Razor added.

Desmond looked at his two buddies.

Lenny nodded, as Infinity had expected.

Motormouth said, "We're using alien technology no one under-
stands to jump to a predator-heavy world. For the freakin' life of
me, you guys, I can't imagine what could go wrong."

Desmond turned to Infinity and nodded. "It's on."

Razor stood up. "Drink at least a quart of water before you turn
in. At least another quart in the morning, no later than 6:00 AM.
Once the water is in your cells and bloodstream, it's yours. Bridging
won't take it from you. It's possible we won't drink water for the
entire thirty-six hours. If you're still hungry, eat now. By morning,
most of the food will be absorbed. Don't bother eating breakfast. If
bridging didn't take it from you, you'd probably purge it."

To Infinity's surprise, he took the time to shake each tourist's
hand. This was her first time partnering with Razor on an excursion, so she wasn't familiar with his habits. As he shook their hands,
he looked each of them in the eye and said, "Godspeed, tourist. The
bridgers have your back." He then left the room, no doubt headed
for his own private pre-bridge rituals.

Infinity was suddenly aware that she had never spoken much to
tourists during briefings. No reason to change now. She simply
nodded at them and walked out.

INFINITY STARED at the most beautiful night sky she'd ever seen.
Streaks of purple and green faded and brightened, wavering about

like glowing shocks of hair blowing in the breeze. She blinked away a drop of sweat that had run into her eye. Every one of her muscles strained to keep her body rigid. Her arms were between her legs, holding her body elevated above the picnic table. Her legs extended horizontally in the air in front of her. It was called the firefly pose, and it was good for maintaining core strength. But it was also an effective tool for clearing the mind, although the amazing sky before her was distracting.

Her muscles were starting to burn. She took a deep breath and stared at the wavering lights. And then she heard footsteps approaching on the grass, breaking her focus. She relented and lowered herself to the tabletop. She hadn't expected company this late, so she had removed her clothes. After years of bridging, she was more relaxed without them.

"That's impressive." It was the tourist, Desmond. "I'm sorry if I interrupted."

"You did," she said.

"Well, I'm sorry. Did you know it's midnight? Shouldn't you be getting some sleep?"

"Don't worry about me."

He sat on the tabletop next to her and put his feet on the bench. "I couldn't sleep either. Too nervous, I guess."

She ignored him and started winding down her workout with some stretches.

He looked up to the northern sky. "Beautiful, isn't it?" He paused. "But it scares the crap out of me."

She looked at him, surprised. "Why's that?"

"This is the first time I've been to Missouri, but I'm pretty sure auroras are rare here, if not unheard of."

She looked at the shimmering colors. "Until now."

"Auroras happen when solar wind interacts with the Earth's magnetosphere. In order for them to start happening in places this far from the north polar region, something would have to disrupt the planet's magnetic field. It's like the world is just falling apart."

Infinity didn't often waste time thinking about weather, or earthquakes, or anything else in the news for that matter. She had a job she was good at, and it paid well. The world's concerns were not hers.

She finished the extension stretches of her right leg and switched to the left. "Well, like you said, it's beautiful."

He let out a half-hearted laugh, and then she sensed that he was staring at her. It pissed her off, but it was probably a good thing that he was. On the job, when clothes weren't an option, there was no place for gawking. But in a situation like this, there was something dishonest about a guy who pretended not to notice when she was naked. "Watch your gaze, tourist."

He turned away. "Sorry. I was just looking at your tattoo. It's nice. I recognize the bird, a painted bunting. I just... well, you don't strike me as a bird-tattoo kind of person. A scorpion or rattlesnake, maybe."

She turned and glared at him.

"Well," he said, "I do like it, just so you know. It must be fresh. In the daylight earlier I saw redness around it."

She paused her stretching and put one hand to the tattoo on her chest. "It's fresh and it's not. This is the fourth time it's been re-inked. I lose some of the ink each time I bridge." Desmond didn't have any tattoos that Infinity had seen, so that was one thing he wouldn't have to worry about.

"I imagine that must get expensive."

Infinity didn't have much else to spend her money on. If she survived bridging for another year or two, she planned to quit and do something normal. But this was none of the tourist's business, so she didn't answer.

He sighed and stepped down from the picnic table. Maybe he was finally getting the message that she was busy.

"Obviously I've never bridged before," he said. "Does the process hurt?"

"It can."

"I've been excited about it for weeks. But I haven't let myself be afraid yet. Should I?"

She went back to stretching, working on her left arm. "Not tonight. You need sleep. Remember, you'll have two bridgers with you."

He stood there gazing at her, the green and red glow from the sky reflecting off his face, making it hard not to stare back at him. Finally, he turned and headed back the way he'd come.

"I hope you sleep well, Infinity," he said over his shoulder.

She released her arm and watched him walk away. He paused for a moment to gaze at the colors in the sky. Then he shook his head and entered the SafeTrek compound.

She started on her right arm. "Yeah, you too," she said softly.

4

COUNTDOWN

August 3

DESMOND HAD BEEN awake for some time when his alarm went off at 5:50 AM, ten minutes before one of the techs was supposed to escort him to the bridging chamber. He hadn't planned on needing more than ten minutes to get ready. There was no point in showering—supposedly the dirt on his skin would be removed during the bridge. And no point shaving—he'd lose all his hair too.

No sooner had he turned the alarm off, than he heard a gentle knocking on the door. The tech was early. Desmond sighed and got up from the bed, still wearing the clothes he'd worn the day before. "One second," he said. He looked in the mirror and tightened the disheveled band on his ponytail. Might as well have it looking halfway neat one more time before losing it altogether. He stepped to the door and opened it.

The tech was there, but so were Lenny and Xavier, as well as Armando Doyle's assistant, Celia Pickett.

Lenny tilted his head toward Celia. "She wants to tell us all something before we head for Dimension X."

Desmond moved aside, and they all entered his room. The tech, a thin guy in his forties maybe and wearing cotton scrubs, stood to the side with his arms crossed. Lenny and Xavier looked like they hadn't gotten any more sleep than Desmond had. They each held a half-finished one-liter water bottle, which reminded Desmond that he was supposed to hydrate. He grabbed his bottle from beside his bed.

As usual, Celia got right to the point. "Mr. Doyle asked me to deliver some breaking news he thought you three would find interesting." She hesitated briefly like she wanted to make sure they were listening. "As I'm sure you know, since the discovery of the Outlander's radio signal five years ago, scientists' efforts to survey more segments of the sky have multiplied. Well, last night SETI announced that a second source of non-natural radio signals has been discovered."

Desmond was suddenly alert.

Xavier spoke first. "A second source? You mean from the Outlanders?"

Celia shook her head. "Not from the Outlanders. From a source almost forty-two degrees distant from the Outlanders."

"Hot damn." Lenny said.

"Another civilization, then?" Xavier asked.

"Possibly, but also possibly not. The second signal uses the same formatting protocols used by the Outlanders. Either the Outlanders have colonized another world at a staggering distance from the source of the first signal, or another civilization has used the same signal formatting."

"Perhaps another civilization also discovered the first signal and decided to rebroadcast it." Desmond said.

She nodded. "That's possible as well, but preliminary checks

indicate the signals contain different information. At least this time
they can decode the signal in hours, rather than months."

Xavier glanced at his watch. "And we're bridging in less than an
hour. I guess we'll have to wait until we get back tomorrow night to
find out what it says." He blew out a long breath and shook
his head.

Lenny slapped Xavier and Desmond on their backs. "Never
been a better time to be alive, brothers. Biggest mind-screwing
period in human history."

Celia turned toward the door. "We almost decided to forego
burdening you with such momentous news just before your excursion. But Mr. Doyle is quite excited about it. He wanted you to
know. He is hopeful that the new signal will provide additional
information on bridging technology." She half-smiled, the first time
Desmond had seen anything but seriousness on her face. "I think
he would like to believe that this second civilization received the
first signal before we did, and they have discovered the missing
hows and whys and are attempting to share the knowledge with
others." She rolled her eyes, smiling, giving Desmond the impression she had playfully teased Doyle about this. "I'll see you in a few
minutes." She left the room.

The tech placed a black rectangular case on the desk next to
Desmond's bed and popped it open, revealing three filled syringes
and three small bottles. "Gentlemen, if you're ready, we must
administer the tagging radioisotope as close to 6:00 AM as possible.
And then I'll take you to the bridging chamber." He held up one of
the syringes. "Who's first?"

Desmond stepped forward.

As the tech swabbed alcohol on Desmond's arm, he explained,
"This is a special cocktail of carriers and the radioisotope, tech-
netium-99m. We administer it both orally and by injection an hour
before bridging to give it ample time to distribute itself throughout
your body. Due to a unique prepping process, the radioisotope will

not begin to decay until the bridging device scans your body, which happens at almost the exact instant of bridging." He jabbed the needle in without warning and quickly emptied the syringe. "Technetium-99m has a half-life of slightly more than six hours. When it decays to the exact point where there is 1.56% remaining, the bridging device pulls you back to our world. That gives you precisely thirty-six hours and 3.6 seconds to enjoy your excursion." He smiled broadly and handed Desmond one of the small bottles. "Please drink this."

Lenny stepped forward for his dose. "What if we're five miles away from where we entered the other world?"

"Doesn't seem to matter. It'll pull you back from wherever you are."

Lenny grunted as the needle entered his arm. "Let me guess, you have no idea how it does that."

The guy smiled again. "Perhaps we'll get all the answers soon." He then laughed and shook his head. Apparently he was as skeptical as Celia regarding Doyle's theory.

A few minutes later the radioisotope dosing was complete, and the tech led them to the bridging chamber. They passed through an airlock that had both hatches hanging open, and then they walked through a well-equipped lab area.

"This is where you'll spend three enjoyable days when you return, going through patho- and chemo-cleansing." The tech turned and gave them a wry smile. "It's also where we evaluate bioprobe animals and treat client and bridger injuries."

Xavier said, "Should I ask how often people return with injuries, or do I even want to know?"

The tech turned and glanced at them. "Some excursions are worse than others. There's a direct correlation between frequency of injuries and how far back you choose your point of divergence."

"That's terrific," Xavier said.

"That's what makes this whole zip-banging excursion exciting," Lenny said. "Man-up, Xavier."

They passed through a second airlock—also with open hatches —into the bridging chamber itself. Celia and four other techs were already in the chamber, but the bridgers weren't there yet. Desmond's eyes were drawn to the plastic-covered, cushioned floor. The techs had done a good job of cleaning the stains from the bio-probe animals returning dead or injured the previous evening, but the center area of the floor was permanently stained dark, probably from countless returning bio-probes—maybe even people.

While the techs took readings of blood pressure, body tempera-ture, and various other parameters, Desmond, Lenny, and Xavier made small talk until Infinity and Razor entered the chamber at 6:45. Razor shook their hands again and said things like, "You're about to see things no human has seen," and "Ready for the ulti-mate adventure?" Infinity, on the other hand, stood against a wall of the chamber stretching her arms and legs with her eyes closed. Desmond wondered if that was part of her ritual.

Celia had her tablet, and she looked at it before speaking. "Mr. Doyle couldn't be here to see you off. He's flying to California to forcefully insert himself into the efforts to decode the new extrater-restrial signals. So I'll be providing your last-minute instructions. Infinity and Razor, please clarify anything I may miss." She looked at her tablet again. "Since you haven't bridged before, it is likely the process will be disorienting. It's possible you'll feel some nausea immediately following the bridge."

"What she means is you're gonna throw up," Razor said. "Nine out of ten tourists do. Don't let it dampen your spirits or break your focus."

Celia went on. "We have found that when bridging to worlds with more distant divergence points, you may arrive there above the ground, similar to what you saw when the bio-probe animals returned. We assume this is some kind of built-in safety feature of the bridging device, to compensate for increased uncertainty of the other world's terrain."

"So just before we bridge," Razor added, "make sure you're standing upright with your feet firmly under you but with your knees slightly bent. The idea is to land on your feet and absorb the shock of the fall."

Celia said, "Your bridgers are experts at this. Keep in mind that the first few minutes are crucial. They'll follow a standard protocol in those first few minutes in order to minimize any possible risks to the three of you."

Razor clarified. "What she's saying is that you need to follow our orders, both promptly and without question. Once we've determined there's no immediate danger, you can begin to explore. But not until then. Agreed?"

Desmond, Lenny, and Xavier all nodded.

"Thank you, Razor," Celia said. She then turned to the tourists. "That's it. We like to keep our pre-bridging instructions simple. Your bridgers will provide additional information on an as-needed basis." She looked at one of the techs. "Any physiological issues?"

He shook his head. "Everything is within normal ranges."

She thanked him, and then he and the other techs left the chamber.

Celia pointed to five empty, plastic, zippered bags that had been left on the floor. "Your clothing."

Infinity and Razor had come to the chamber barefoot, but they immediately began pulling off their shorts and t-shirts.

Celia seemed to recognize that Desmond, Lenny, and Xavier were hesitant, and she turned her back to them. "Just place the bags beside me when you're done."

Desmond and Lenny began removing their clothes, but Xavier removed only his watch. He placed it into his bag and put it next to Celia's feet.

"You do know the clothes aren't going with you," Infinity said.

"I don't mind losing them," he replied, "for a few more minutes of dignity."

Razor put a hand on Xavier's shoulder. "Here's the real deal. You can lose your clothes if you want to, but bridging with clothes on causes a burning sensation on your skin as the clothes are stripped away. No idea why."

Xavier looked at him and then glanced at Celia. He sighed, removed his clothes, and added them to his bag.

Celia gathered up the five bags and stepped to the hatch. She turned around and gazed at Xavier for several seconds with a slightly mischievous smile. Finally, she said. "Good luck. I can scarcely imagine the wondrous things you'll see. Thirty-six hours can pass quickly. Enjoy every minute of it." She stepped through the hatch and closed it behind her.

Razor actually chuckled out loud, and Desmond realized he and Celia were having fun at Xavier's expense.

"Very funny," Xavier said. "Do you guys do that to everyone, or only when your boss is out of town?"

This made Razor laugh even harder.

Desmond looked at Infinity. She shook her head without cracking a smile.

"Stand in the middle of the room," she said. "Two feet of space between everyone."

They all gathered there as instructed. Desmond realized his heart was pounding. He tried breathing slowly, but it didn't help.

Celia's voice came through a speaker somewhere. "Two minutes."

Desmond turned to the largest of the plexiglass windows. Celia and two of the techs were seated on the other side, watching them.

"Just relax," Razor said in a calm voice. "It helps to think about something you like. For me, it's skydiving."

Really, Desmond thought, that's what calms him down? He

tried to focus on one of his favorite hiking trails near his home in Kentucky.

"One minute," Celia announced.

Infinity tapped Desmond's shoulder. "Move your feet apart. Now bend your knees. Lenny, get those knees bent, like you're about to land after jumping."

"Hold your arms out at an angle," Razor said. "It helps your balance, and it facilitates the body scan."

"Thirty seconds."

"Remember," Infinity said, "we're here to protect and assist. The first minutes are critical. Do what we say, when we say it."

Several more seconds passed.

"Here we go, baby!" Lenny said.

"Ten seconds."

Desmond thought of fresh forest air and a breeze whispering through the trees.

"Five, four, three, two, one."

5

BRIDGE

August 3 — 7:00 AM

FOR JUST AN INSTANT, Desmond felt wet and prickly, like he'd been wrapped in a slimy cactus. And then he was falling. He hit the ground hard. His legs buckled and one of his knees slammed into his face. His nose exploded with pain. He rolled on the ground, clutching his face.

Someone shouted, "Aw goddammit, my leg!"

"Severe placement error! Assess and give me a plan, Razor. I'll check injuries."

Razor responded immediately. "Open rocky hillside. Forest down-slope at two hundred yards. No other cover near."

Someone pulled Desmond's hands from his face. Infinity stared down at him. "Anything broken besides your nose, tourist? Try to stand up." She turned and was gone.

Desmond looked at his hands, covered in blood.

"No large animals visible," Razor said. "Flocks of birds in the distance. Best option: move to the forest now."

"Be careful!" Xavier's voice was desperate. "Oh Jesus, look at it."

"Fractured tibia," Infinity said. "Possibly more."

Desmond turned to look. Infinity was squatting beside Xavier, but she quickly got up and moved to Lenny.

"I'm okay," he said. He got to his knees and stood up.

She turned back to Desmond. "I said can you get up? Move!"

He grunted and sat up. Blood flowed freely from his face onto his legs and groin. Suddenly, Razor's outstretched hand was in his face. Desmond grabbed it, and the bridger pulled him up.

"I think my legs are okay," he said.

"Good," Infinity said. "We're moving to the forest. Don't get ahead of us or fall behind. We all stay in a tight group." She and Razor pulled Xavier up onto one foot.

Xavier cried out. His broken foot swung loosely from a point halfway up the calf. The sight made Desmond's chest tighten. He forced himself to look away. He realized suddenly that this would change everything about the excursion.

"I know it hurts," Razor said as he and Infinity got on each side and put Xavier's arms over their shoulders. "But we're taking you down the slope. I want you to muster everything you've got to stop yourself from yelling. We need to be discreet."

Xavier made an almost inhuman groan, possibly trying to convey that he would try.

"You guys," Lenny said, gazing up the slope behind them. "I know you may be preoccupied right now, but there's a wicked-awesome example of the local wildlife right up there."

Desmond turned and followed his gaze. The creature was silhouetted against the blue sky, so he couldn't see color or fine details. But it was bird-like, standing on two legs. It appeared to be as tall as an ostrich, but with a thicker neck and legs, and a much larger head. A thin, wispy fringe outlined its body against the sky—feathers or perhaps fur.

The creature crouched lower, as if it had suddenly realized it'd been spotted. It leaned forward and began walking, skirting to the side of the humans. Its movements were smooth and restrained, indicating it could move much faster if it wanted to. As it moved down the slope, coming closer, Desmond saw that it was brown, about the color of a deer or coyote.

"That's a predator," Infinity said, her voice lower than it had been moments before. "Let's move. Stay tight—try to look like one large animal."

She and Razor started down the hill, Xavier stifling pained grunts.

Desmond couldn't take his eyes off the creature—it was unlike anything he'd ever seen. Another movement caught his eye. A second creature of the same type coming over the hilltop. And then another to the side of that one. Seconds later, two more appeared. As they appeared, each one, mimicking the first, stared for a moment and then crouched and began skirting the humans. Two of them moved toward the first one, but the remaining two went in the other direction.

Desmond's neck tingled, although it no longer had hair that could stand up. He rushed to join the others. "There are at least five of them now, and it looks to me like they're stalking us."

Infinity and Razor looked over their shoulders and then at each other.

"Okay," Infinity said. "Desmond and Lenny, watch them as we move. Tell us if their behavior changes in any way. When we get to the trees, first grab anything you can wield as a weapon. Long spears are better, remember, but there's no time to grind tips. Second, climb a tree. The higher the better. Take your weapons up with you."

The bird-like creatures were now alongside them, about fifty yards out on each side. The animals were definitely stalking them. The forest was still a hundred yards away.

Razor pointed at the ground with his free hand. "Lenny, give me that rock."

Without slowing down, Lenny leaned over, snagged it, and handed it to Razor.

"Now grab one for yourself. Desmond, do the same. If they get close, throw. Pick up another rock as soon as you throw."

Infinity said, "If they keep coming, make a lot of noise and hold your hands up to look bigger. Give me one of those rocks."

Desmond spotted two small enough to pick up, grabbed them one after the other, stumbling a bit after the second, and put one into her free hand. Xavier was now grunting and moaning uncontrollably. Lenny looked at Desmond with wide eyes and gestured toward the bird creatures, like he couldn't believe this was happening. The predators were still alongside them but hadn't come within throwing distance. The creatures were moving low to the ground, and every few seconds they turned their heads and looked directly at the five humans.

Fifty yards to the forest. Desmond realized the trees weren't like any he'd ever seen. They had green structures at the branch tips, but they looked nothing like leaves. Instead, they were round, semi-translucent orbs about the size of a baseball. The twigs they were attached to were only a few inches long. And those were attached to thicker branches no more than two feet long. These in turn were attached to two-foot branches connecting to the main trunk, which resembled a green, upside-down carrot. These branches would be totally useless as spears.

When they finally arrived at the forest edge, the bird creatures were still maintaining their distance. The forest was bordered by smaller, brushy plants, all of them with green orbs for leaves. They pushed their way through the brush and into the forest.

The sunlight beneath the trees had a strange, green hue from passing through the bubble leaves. Desmond looked to one side to see what the creatures would do. They moved silently and gracefully among the trees, now coming directly toward the humans. He looked in the other direction—the others were doing the same, as if they'd been waiting for the humans to enter the forest.

Infinity was watching the predators, too. "Pick a tree and climb, now!"

Desmond didn't need to be told twice. Fortunately, the trees were easy to climb, with thick branches growing near the ground. The green trunk was surprisingly soft to the touch, but this didn't impede their climbing. He and Lenny were ten feet up before Desmond turned to look down.

Infinity and Razor had taken Xavier to the base of another tree, but it was too late to help him up. The creatures were less than ten yards away and steadily creeping closer.

Infinity and Razor stood shoulder to shoulder with their backs to him, each of them armed only with a jagged rock. "Climb with your arms and good leg," Infinity instructed Xavier.

Xavier grunted and sobbed, trying to pull himself up.

One of the creatures broke away from the others and darted over to Desmond and Lenny's tree. It stood beneath them, looking up with large, round eyes and circular pupils. Its head was the size and general shape of a large dog's but with a thick beak almost ten inches long instead of a muzzle. And Desmond now noticed that the creatures had forelimbs. They were small, like those of a velociraptor, with long, clawed fingers.

Lenny threw his rock, striking the creature's neck and sending it scampering back.

Four of the creatures were still circling Xavier and the bridgers. They crept confidently, like they might attack any second. "Higher!" Infinity shouted at Xavier, although he was obviously doing the best he could.

"Shock and awe, on my lead," Infinity said.

"Damn right," Razor replied. "You take the head, I got the feet."

Were they really going to try to fight the creatures with their bare hands?

"Climb, Xavier!" Desmond shouted.

The creatures stopped circling and crouched, preparing to lunge at the two naked, seemingly helpless humans.

Infinity screamed savagely and thrust her arms out, hurling her rock at the nearest creature's face. In a blur of motion she kicked the thing in the side of its head as it was trying to avoid the rock. Then she was all over it, knocking it to the ground, her legs encircling its chest until her feet locked together. She clamped her arms around its head, trying to hold its beak shut, and attacked one of its eyes with her teeth.

Razor circled to the back of the animal, threw himself over the body, and grabbed the hind legs. He wrestled with the flailing limbs, keeping the claws away from Infinity.

The other creatures seemed startled by this vicious, coordinated attack, and they nearly stumbled over their own feet trying to back off. They stopped at ten yards out and watched, ready to run if necessary. The restrained creature began screeching, and the others backed off even more.

This was a crucial moment, and Desmond saw a chance to help. Still holding his own rock, he descended to the ground. "I'll kill you!" he screamed, and he rushed at the nearest creature and threw the rock.

This was apparently the tipping point, because two of them turned and ran back out of the forest.

"Get back up in the tree, tourist!" Infinity ordered, her strained voice barely audible above the shrieks of the creature beneath her.

The two remaining predators began creeping toward Desmond, their bodies held low to the ground.

He rushed back to the tree and climbed until he was next to Lenny again.

The predators came to the tree's base and looked up.

"Break its damn neck," Razor snarled.

With her legs still locked around its body, Infinity pulled back harder on the creature's head. "I'm trying!"

Suddenly the two creatures below Desmond and Lenny began climbing. They gripped the branches with their beaks and hind feet, quickly maneuvering themselves upward like parrots.

"You've gotta be kidding," Lenny said.

A rush of panic overtook Desmond. The creatures had evolved to climbing these trees. No wonder they had been in no rush to attack earlier.

"Climb, you guys!" Xavier called out from his own tree.

They climbed, but the predators didn't stop. At twenty yards up, Desmond and Lenny ran out of tree. Seconds later the two creatures were within reach. Rather than rapidly snapping at Desmond and Lenny's feet, the beaked creatures carefully and deliberately opened their jaws and reached upward, following the movement of the humans' feet with their round eyes.

"Jesus, this can't be real," Lenny said as he kicked at the gaping beaks with his bare foot.

Desmond kicked too, knocking one of the beaks to the side but not deterring the creature's efforts.

Suddenly one of the creatures caught Lenny's foot. It then began backing down the tree. Lenny cried out as he started sliding down with it. Desmond grabbed his arm and desperately held on.

Lenny's terror-filled eyes caught Desmond's. "Don't let go, Des!"

The other creature latched onto Lenny's leg just below the knee. The weight of both predators tore Lenny from Desmond's grip. They dragged him down, his arms and head violently striking branches all the way to the ground. The two creatures immediately began dragging away his now-limp body.

"Lenny!" Desmond began climbing down. From the corner of his vision he saw Infinity and Razor get up and rush to Lenny's aide. The creature they'd been holding kept kicking, but it didn't get up.

Desmond jumped past the last few branches. One of Lenny's attackers was running away. The other was in a life-and-death struggle with the two bridgers. Infinity had a solid grip on its head, but Razor was struggling to contain its thrashing feet. Razor was red with blood, but there was no telling if it was his or the creature's.

"I'm letting go," Infinity cried. "Get back!"

Razor scrambled back, and Infinity released the head and rolled away. The creature got to its feet and took off for the open hillside.

Razor collapsed onto his butt, holding his blood-soaked abdomen.

Infinity was already at Lenny's side. Desmond rushed over to them. He stared down in horror at the condition of Lenny's leg. It was completely shredded, much worse than Xavier's fracture. His foot hardly resembled a foot at all. The creatures' beaks must have been unimaginably powerful to do such damage.

Infinity slapped Lenny's face. "Wake up, tourist. I need you to focus."

Lenny moaned, barely conscious.

Infinity swiveled her head to look at Razor, who was still sitting, clutching his belly. Then she glanced up at Xavier, still in his tree. She stood up and faced Desmond. "Listen to me, tourist. Priorities have changed. Forget whatever purpose you came here for. We have a new purpose—survival. We're here until 7:00 PM tomorrow night. At that point we can bridge back alive or as heaps of half-digested goo. I prefer alive. All of us. Understood?"

Desmond was shaking and didn't trust himself to speak, so he just nodded.

"We have severe injuries, but right now priority one is defense. We have to make safety our number one priority."

He wiped the blood from his throbbing nose and flicked it to the ground. "Okay, what can I do?"

"We need concealment. And weapons."

6

SHELTER

Infinity's strength was starting to fade. The tourist, Lenny, was fading in and out of consciousness, so she had resorted to a fireman's carry. She was slick with sweat, and so was the tourist, which made it even harder to hold on to his naked body. They had trekked perhaps a half-mile without seeing anything that would provide a place to hide or any debris that could be fashioned into weapons. And the forest of bubble-trees was only getting thicker. At least two of the predators were still following them, hanging back a hundred yards, perhaps hoping for them to leave behind one of the wounded.

Ahead and to the left she saw a brighter area, possibly a clearing. Any change in the terrain was worth checking out, so she veered left. Razor and the other tourists were lagging behind, so she paused. It was critical for everyone to stay together.

Razor and Desmond supported Xavier, at this point just dragging him along. Xavier was conscious but was exhausted from hopping on one foot. Razor's face showed no signs of pain, but his labored grunts and staggering stride told a different story. He was in bad shape. If the predator's claws had penetrated an inch deeper, they would have spilled his guts. As it was, he was losing blood fast.

"Keep going," Razor grunted as the three of them caught up.

Lenny moaned as Infinity hefted his body higher on her shoulders for the hundredth time. They all trudged on.

Soon they emerged into the clearing. It seemed to have been created when several large trees had fallen, knocking over additional smaller trees. The trees had fallen into two main piles. Their fleshy green parts had rotted away, revealing woody structural trunks, like skeletons. Chest-high green stalks were growing nearby in several clusters, and they looked rigid. Possibly rigid enough to be useful.

"I'm putting you down," Infinity said as she took a knee and rolled Lenny off to one side.

Lenny moaned again, still barely conscious.

Infinity stood up and faced the others. "We're stopping here. It's the best place for shelter we've seen." She pointed to the larger of the two piles of tree skeletons. "That's our starting point. I think we can all fit beneath it. We'll use the trees from the other pile to reinforce it. Razor, can you work?"

He nodded. "Damn right."

"You and Desmond get the wounded inside there. Then start reinforcing the structure. I'll go search for something we can use to make weapons."

She scanned the forest, pausing her gaze in the direction they'd just come. She had seen movement—brown shapes slinking smoothly among the trees. But she couldn't tell how many. She scanned the ground. Rocks were plentiful but mostly buried, probably difficult to remove. She shoved one with her bare foot, confirming this. She shoved another. The second one moved, so she worked it free with her hands and tossed it near the jumble of tree trunks. She gathered three more and placed them beside the first.

Razor and Desmond had already moved Lenny's limp body

into the interior of the pile of logs and branches, and now they were helping Xavier crawl through the jumbled branches. He whimpered and huffed but didn't cry out. He was proving to be tougher than he looked. Assuming Lenny didn't have a severe concussion or other damage they couldn't see, and assuming they weren't killed by predators in the next thirty-four hours, the two injured tourists would survive until bridge-back. It was surprising what the body could endure for a day and a half, especially if antibiotics, medical equipment, and good surgeons were available upon returning.

Infinity moved to the center of the clearing to inspect the stalks growing there. The first thing she noticed was that swarms of insects were buzzing around the three or four greenish balls at the top of each stalk. Like the weird leaves on the trees, each of the balls was bigger than her fist, and she could see right through them. She squeezed one between her fingers until it burst. The air around it immediately smelled sweet, and dozens of insects swooped in from the other stalks, hovering there as if sucking in the aroma. Interesting, but not useful.

She gripped one of the stalks and wrenched it from the ground. It had a fleshy surface like the larger trees, but there had to be something hard inside for the stalks to stand erect. She took the stalk to the rocks she'd dug up. It didn't take long to grind the end of it down between two of them. She had been right—the center was dense, and it held a good point.

She smiled to herself for the first time since bridging to this world.

INFINITY FOUND what she had been looking for, a low area with a small stream. Luckily it was within eyesight of Razor and the tourists.

Unfortunately, the stalking predators were also within eyesight.

The damn things had gradually moved closer to the crude shelter. And now more had arrived. She had counted at least eight, but she couldn't be sure because they kept moving, weaving back and forth between the trees in a way that made her nerves raw. If this behavior was a strategy to drive their prey to panic, then it was effective. The tourist Xavier had become fixated on it. Razor had finally put Xavier to work grinding points on the plant stalks, which seemed to be shutting him up.

Infinity didn't want the stream for its water. She and the others would drink only if necessary. Hornet had told her once about a tourist getting violently sick within minutes of drinking water on a world with a divergence far more recent than this one. Different plants and animals meant different soil. Different soil meant different groundwater. No, what she needed was mud.

She stepped into the water, and her bare foot sank several inches into the streambed. Perfect. She scanned the area to make sure the predators weren't approaching, and then she scooped up mud and began smearing it over her skin, quickly covering every inch of her body. It immediately soothed the insect bites she'd sustained. Like the water, the insects here could be different. So different, in fact, that their bites could be highly toxic. A layer of mud on the skin would keep most of them from biting. She gathered as much as she could carry and went back to the others.

Razor and Desmond had done a decent job of carrying logs from the smaller pile and using them to reinforce the shelter. With the supporting logs wedged into place, there were only a few holes, which were big enough for a human to fit through but too small for the predators that were stalking them. The shelter's biggest weakness was the top. They didn't have enough logs to close it off completely.

Lenny was now out of his semiconscious stupor and was sitting up with the others within the shelter. "That's a good look for you,

Infinity," he said as she approached. This idiotic comment was a good sign that he hadn't suffered a serious head injury.

Ignoring him, she leaned into one of the shelter's openings and dumped her load of mud at their feet. "Spread this on yourselves. Leave nothing exposed, not even your open wounds."

Xavier looked up at her, his face pale from blood loss or shock. "Are you crazy? I can't put mud on this." He nodded down at his fractured leg, which was tinted deep shades of black and blue.

"Yes you can. You'll be patho-cleansed when we bridge back. The mud will hide your scent, and it's decent camouflage. Plus, it'll stop the biting insects. If that's not reason enough, think of it as putting on clothing." She turned to go get another armload. But then she froze.

Their situation had reached whatever tipping point the predators had been waiting for. They were coming—and fast. Infinity crawled through an opening to the interior of the shelter and jammed two short branches in place to close it off.

"Good God," Lenny said. "It's a killer bird convention."

Infinity peeked through the maze of limbs. There were now at least fifteen predators—no wonder they'd decided to attack. She grabbed the sharpened stalks and handed them out to the others. "Position yourself so you can use both hands. Thrust hard—into the eyes or mouth. Push like you're trying to break through the back of the skull. If they try to claw you through the openings, grab their feet and pull. Then I'll—"

The predators suddenly jumped onto the pile of dead trees, shaking the entire shelter. The tourists began shouting and jabbing wildly.

The creatures covered the shelter, scrabbling over each other and tearing at the logs with their beaks, tossing aside the smaller sticks and ripping pieces off the larger branches.

Infinity thrust her weapon into an open beak, feeling a satisfying impact with soft tissue and then bone. The creature screeched and retreated but came right back.

A long leg came in through one of the gaps, its claws nearly impaling Infinity's face. Desmond shot his hand out and grabbed one of its toes. He quickly pulled back on it, bracing his feet against the logs.

"I've got it!" He cried.

Infinity rammed her weapon into the predator's abdomen with all her strength. It went deep. She tried yanking it out, but the creature twisted and squirmed, pulling its leg from Desmond's grip and breaking the sharpened stalk. The predator fell back, writhing on the ground.

"Hit the abdomen, between the legs!" Infinity shouted.

At that moment a predator's head and neck came through a gap above Xavier, beak open and darting straight for his head. Razor flipped his stalk around and jabbed it sideways with one hand, piercing the creature's eye. Razor pushed harder and the stalk made a sickening crunch as it broke through the back of the eye socket, and the creature went limp. Razor pulled the stalk out and the head hung loosely above Xavier's.

"And hit the eyes!" Infinity cried as she stabbed again and again.

Another head came through and was stabbed by three sharpened stalks at once.

But the creatures kept coming. With a series of loud cracks, another hole appeared above Infinity, and the entire ceiling sagged under the creatures' weight.

"Don't wear your arms out," Razor said, his voice much calmer than Infinity's. "Aim and thrust, aim and thrust." He shoved his weapon in rhythm with the words, each thrust wounding another predator.

The tourists followed his lead and slowed their pace. But Infinity could see it was a losing battle. The predators weren't easy to kill, and they didn't give up when injured. She looked around frantically, her mind racing to come up with a new plan. But besides defending their quickly-failing shelter, the only other option was to climb the trees. That'd already proven to be imperfect, but they had to do something. The creatures were still concentrating their attack on one side of the shelter, leaving the backside clear. She could see no other option but to lure the predators away long enough to give the tourists a chance to get up into the trees. She couldn't outrun the creatures, so it was probably a suicide move. With any luck, the flesh of her own body would keep them busy long enough. All she had to do was get all of them to chase her at once.

"They're coming in!" Xavier cried. He and Lenny were desperately stabbing at a predator that was halfway through an opening it had created. It caught Lenny's stalk in its beak and ripped it from his hands. Razor pushed his way between the tourists and skewered the predator's neck while Lenny grabbed one of the last remaining weapons.

They were out of time. Infinity pushed her way into a gap in the shelter's backside and started crawling out. A hand clamped onto her ankle and dragged her back in.

"The hell you will," Razor snarled. "I'm already weak. You'll be more useful to them." He moved to the gap and started through it.

She grabbed his arm. "I'm not letting you—"

He turned on her viciously. "No, fuck that! You know I'm right. It's my move. Make it count."

She gritted her teeth but then nodded and handed him the last sharpened stalk. "Kill as many as you can."

"Damn right." He took the extra weapon and crawled through the gap.

Suddenly the predators stopped attacking.

Lenny said, "Are you guys seeing this?"

Infinity turned. The predators were all frozen in place, staring at three approaching creatures. These animals were larger—much larger, each of them the size of two or three adult grizzly bears. Like the smaller predators, they walked upright on two bird legs, and they were covered in brown fur or perhaps feathers. Their diminutive forelimbs were the size of Infinity's arms, and their heads were larger than a horse's, with massive serrated beaks. All three of the beasts stopped and gazed down at the frozen predators with huge, round, unblinking eyes.

"Everyone freeze," Infinity whispered. She then realized Razor was still pushing himself out through the logs behind her, unaware of what was happening. "Razor," she hissed. "Get back in here."

He turned to look.

One of the giants walked around the shelter. It stood above Razor, staring down at him, its head shifting back and forth as if trying to see better.

Suddenly all hell broke loose. The shelter's roof crashed inward. The dead predator with its head hanging down was mashed into the ground between Xavier and Lenny. It was then yanked upward and pulled completely out of the destroyed shelter. Infinity saw movement from the side as another of the giants lunged forward and grabbed one of the smaller predators by the neck. It shook the creature, instantly killing it. The remaining predators scattered.

Infinity turned to Razor. He was holding perfectly still as the third giant, still above him, watched the chaos, swiveling its head like it was trying to decide which retreating predator to chase. But then it turned its attention back to Razor. It leaned forward, extending its massive beak toward him.

Infinity lunged into the tangled branches, trying to get close enough to stab at the giant with her weapon. Several branches cracked, drawing the giant's attention, but she couldn't get through.

Razor took advantage of this distraction and started pushing himself back toward the shelter's interior. This movement caught the giant's eye.

Infinity screamed at it, struggling to get through the tangle with her weapon.

The creature crashed its beak through the branches and grabbed Razor's head. It started walking backwards, pulling his struggling body out of the shelter.

"No!" Infinity screamed.

The giant's beak clamped shut, crushing Razor's skull. His arms and legs stopped flailing.

"God almighty," Xavier said, and then he started retching.

Infinity stared in disbelief at her dead partner, his body now lying ten feet from the shelter. The giant put one foot on Razor's body and began feeding. She turned away. No time to grieve now. The other two giants were busy feeding on their own prey. And the smaller predators were gone.

She turned to Desmond. "We're moving—now. I got Xavier." She pulled Xavier to his knees. Without bothering to check if the giants were coming for them, she fought her way out of the shelter. She reached back in. "Your hand!" Xavier took her hand and she pulled him out, cracking some of the smaller branches in the process. He grunted in pain but didn't scream—definitely tougher than he looked.

Seconds later Desmond was at her side and they pulled Lenny out.

Infinity glanced at the giants. They were still focused on their meals. She made the mistake of looking at Razor's body, which was now half-consumed. She sucked in a lungful of air and bent over to lift Xavier in a fireman's carry.

"Just hold me up," he whispered. "I'll hop."

She put his arm over her shoulder, and they took off as fast as Xavier could move, followed by Desmond and Lenny, hopping along in the same way.

THE TERRAIN WAS STILL FORESTED but had become rockier in the last few hundred yards, with more ups and downs. But still they hadn't found any natural structures offering safety from predators. They were now resting while Infinity inspected a tree she thought would support the weight of all four humans.

"I don't want to go up in a tree again," Xavier said between wheezes. He had been hopping along on one foot for at least half an hour. He and Lenny were showing signs of exhaustion. Soon they'd have to be carried.

"Doesn't matter what you want," she said. But silently she agreed with him. A tree would be a last resort. Besides, she had glimpsed a tall bluff ahead. Maybe they'd find refuge there.

Infinity appraised Lenny, who was standing on one foot, supported by Desmond. If not for Lenny's mangled leg, Infinity wouldn't have been able to tell them apart. A quarter of a mile back they had crossed another small stream, and they'd taken a few minutes to cover themselves in thick mud. With the mud and their bald heads, the three tourists now looked pretty much the same.

"I've been watching," Desmond said, still panting from assisting his friend. "Haven't seen predators. Flushed some birds. A few smaller ground animals."

Lenny sagged against Desmond's side. His shredded and mud-coated foot was still dripping blood. "Gotta sit down, Des. For a few minutes."

"No," Infinity said. "Stay on your feet. There's a cliff of some kind ahead of us. You gotta make it to that. If there's nothing better there, we'll get you into a tree. Then you can rest."

Lenny raised his head and tried to focus, looking through the trees for the cliff. "Okay, I can do it," he said, although Infinity doubted he could even see it. Lenny turned to look at Desmond. "Sorry man, but I gotta say, this vacation sucks."

Desmond started walking, dragging his friend with him. Infinity walked behind them, dragging Xavier.

"And why does Xavier get the girl?" Lenny said. "I love you, man, but I'd rather—"

"Less talking, more walking," Infinity snapped.

As they approached the rocky bluff, Infinity spotted something that gave her a sliver of hope. Several dark, gaping holes were visible on the cliff face, one of them easily large enough that they could fit inside. The good news—it was on a vertical cliff, safe from predators, at least from those they'd seen so far. The bad news—it was on a vertical cliff. The cavity was about ten feet from the top of a solid-stone bluff that was at least fifty feet high.

She stopped and pointed with her free hand. "That's it. That cave is where we're going."

"Whoa, Nelly," Lenny said.

"Impossible," Xavier said. "Not only impossible—insane."

She ignored them and stared at Desmond until he met her gaze. He frowned, cracking some of the mud drying on his face. But then he nodded slightly.

"She's the bridger," he said. "We gotta trust her."

"Suck it up and let's get moving," Infinity said. They all started walking again.

"Impossible and insane," Xavier muttered.

"Less talking, more walking."

They emerged from the trees. Before them, flowing along the base of the cliff, was a river. The water on their side was clear and shallow with a rocky bed, but it dropped off to a deep channel below the cliff.

Infinity glanced at Desmond. He was watching her, and so were the other two.

She looked up and down the river. Downriver the cliff gradually sloped until it was not much higher than the water, a couple hundred yards away. They could cross the river there, walk up the slope, and figure out a way to drop down to the cave. It would be dangerous, but less dangerous than staying on the ground or in a tree.

"The river changes nothing," she said. She nodded toward the cave. "We're still going up there."

7

ROPE

Crossing the river would be less of a problem than Desmond had thought. He was standing in the deepest part, and it was barely to his waist. The most difficult part was slogging through the mud beneath the slower-moving water of the channel. That, and walking barefoot on the rocks of the shallower water. He made his way back to the shore.

"It's not that deep," he called back to Lenny and Xavier, trying to sound positive. "We can do this. Infinity and I will take you across one at a time." He moved to Lenny's side and then waited for Infinity to help. But she was staring upstream.

"Don't move," she said.

Everyone froze. Her low tone could mean only one thing. Ever so slowly, Desmond turned his head to follow her gaze. Less than a hundred yards upstream, four creatures were silently walking from the forest toward the edge of the river. More followed behind them, appearing one at a time in single file. Their coats were brown with diagonal streaks of black, no doubt to facilitate blending into the shadows and shafts of sunlight in the forest. Like most of the other animals Desmond had seen in this world, these walked on two legs, with tiny forearms protruding from their shoulders. Their legs and necks were thinner, and their heads proportionally smaller, than those of the predators. On their faces were blunt, sparrow-like beaks.

Desmond relaxed. Everything about these creatures suggested that they were timid herbivores, not predators. And the way they paused every few steps to survey their surroundings indicated they preferred to avoid conflict rather than seeking it out. As the creatures arrived at the river's edge, they lowered their heads and began drinking. Soon nearly fifteen of them were lined up by the water, taking turns drinking and watching for danger.

"Those aren't predators," Infinity said, and she moved to Lenny's other side.

One of the creatures spotted the movement. It let out a shrill whistle and stamped one foot on the rocky ground. The other heads shot up to look. And then they all ran, disappearing into the forest.

"Infinity," Lenny said as they guided him into the water, "you need to figure out how tourists can bring cameras through the bridge. Those things were wicked-cool, like this world's version of deer."

As they moved into the deeper water, Lenny looked down. "Man, still bleeding." The water had washed the layer of mud off his leg and mangled foot, and spirals of dark red were swirling away in the current.

"Don't focus on it," Infinity said. "You're not losing enough to die before 7:00 PM tomorrow."

Another movement in the water caught Desmond's eye. A mass of flashing silver moved toward them, apparently following the trail of blood—a school of small fish. They shot forward the last few feet, swarming Lenny's foot.

"What is that?" Lenny said. "Ow. They're biting!"

"Move, tourists!" Infinity picked up the pace, practically dragging them both.

Lenny began jerking his leg back and forth. "Ow! Ouch. Hurry!"

As they pulled him up the far bank, Lenny actually snorted out a laugh. "The little shits are wicked-vicious."

They set him on his butt, and Infinity inspected his leg. She plucked off a three-inch fish that had refused to let go and held it up between her fingers for them to see. It was similar in structure to the fish of their own world. It obviously had feeding habits similar to a piranha's, but it was longer and thinner, like a minnow with teeth.

"I'm not getting in that water," Xavier called out from the other shore.

Infinity tossed the fish aside. "Yes you are." She started back across.

Desmond followed her. "Don't worry Xavier, you won't be in long enough for them to hurt you. Just be glad your crotch isn't bleeding."

Xavier complained a bit more, but they hauled him across, but this time the fish didn't show up. When they were all together on the shore, they re-applied mud to their bodies.

As Infinity finished covering her scalp and face, she said, "Listen up. We need to make a length of rope. We need long plant fibers: grass, reeds, long leaves, stems. Or animal skin, tendons, or guts. Anything long. We'll collect what we can as we make our way up the slope to the cliff ridge." She eyed them for a minute. "Everyone understand?"

Sitting on their butts in the mud, Xavier and Lenny nodded.

Desmond said, "How are *you* doing, Infinity? Razor is dead and you haven't said a word about it."

She gazed at him, but her expression was hard to read beneath the layer of mud. "He's not the first partner I've lost. Doesn't help to talk about it. What matters is that you three are alive. Because of his sacrifice. That's what bridgers do."

They were all silent for several seconds.

"Here's to Razor, then," Lenny said, and he held up an imaginary glass.

"To Razor," Desmond and Xavier said. They leaned in and touched Lenny's hand with their fists. The three tourists turned to Infinity to see if she would join them.

She nodded without holding her hand out. "Damn right."

As they approached the crest of the hill, they found several varieties of grass-like plants that Infinity said would suffice for making rope. They pulled some but couldn't carry much while supporting Xavier and Lenny. By the time they arrived at the spot directly above the cave, they had dropped half of what they'd gathered.

As Desmond lowered Lenny to the ground, he noticed there were no trees or protruding rocks to anchor a rope—one more factor casting doubt on Infinity's plan. But he decided not to dampen the mood by bringing it up. He and Infinity gathered the grass they had dropped and the rest of what was growing in the area, but it wasn't much. They carried it back to Xavier and Lenny.

"Move back from the edge," Infinity said. "You're visible to predators coming to the river to drink." They scooted back, and she sat on the ground between them, the pile of plant fibers in front of her. She picked up a few of the stems and pulled on them, testing their strength. "Watch carefully. I don't want to have to show you twice." She laid a bundle of the grass on a flat stone and pounded it gently with another stone, starting at one end of the bundle and pounding her way to the other end. "This makes it flexible. Don't hit so hard it cuts through the fibers."

She then extracted about twenty stems from the bundle, tied them all in a knot at one end, and separated the loose end into two bundles of about ten stems each. "Watch what I do with my fingers." She twisted one of the bundles of ten several times and then passed it over the second bundle. She did the same to the second bundle, twisting it and then passing it back over the first. "Twist the bundle one direction, then wrap the twisted bundle around the other bundle in the opposite direction. This way it'll bind tighter under a load." Her fingers sped up, twisting and wrapping, twisting and wrapping.

Seconds later only a few inches of the fibers remained unwrapped. "When you get to the end, splice another bundle into each strand." She picked up another bundle of ten and demonstrated the splicing. "Keep doing this until your cord is about twenty feet long. How long, Xavier?"

"I heard you. Twenty feet."

"Good. When you've made at least twenty of those twenty-foot cords, we'll braid them together in the same way but on a larger scale. That'll shorten the whole thing to about fifteen feet. Desmond, why do we need fifteen feet?"

"Because that'll be long enough to reach the cave below us."

"Lenny, why not make it longer than that?"

"Uh, because we can't waste any time?"

"Good." She got to her feet. "You make cords. I'll go look for more fibers. If I don't come back, get it done anyway. Your best chance to survive until bridge-back is to get in that cave." She turned to leave.

Desmond got up. "Wait. I should go instead of you." He nodded toward Lenny and Xavier. "If something attacks, you can protect them better than I can."

She frowned at him. "You're right. You should go. But listen. Predators will either hear you, smell you, or see you. Be aware of that. Move silently. Keep your eyes open, especially downwind. Anything smells you, that's where it'll come from. You can't avoid a predator unless you see it before it sees you. Understood?"

He nodded.

"Go upstream. Stay in sight of the river. You can't get lost that way."

He nodded again. "I don't plan to go far."

He left them on the cliff and headed upstream alone.

———

DESMOND DIDN'T FIND a substantial stand of suitable grasses until he had descended the hill and made his way to the top of the next ridge. The grasses apparently grew only on the hilltops where there were no trees. He pulled all he could find and placed them in a pile. It didn't look like enough. He saw another hilltop another quarter-mile upstream. He turned and looked back the way he'd come. He could see the first ridge but couldn't make out the three humans sitting there. That was good. The less visible they were, the better.

Being this far from the others was already starting to make him uncomfortable. Not only that, but his feet were also bleeding from the rocky terrain. But he couldn't go back without what he'd come for. He left the pile of grass to pick up on his way back and headed down the slope toward the next hill.

A small stream ran through the valley between the two hills, emptying into the river. Desmond stopped long enough to apply a fresh layer of mud to his skin. The mud had become a comfort to him, making him feel less exposed.

As he was climbing the next hill, two creatures exploded from a low clump of brush. Desmond staggered back in panic. But instead of attacking, the creatures fled. They were the same type of timid animals the humans had seen drinking from the river. One was half the size of the other, perhaps a mother and its offspring.

Watching them disappear amidst the trees on the hillside, Desmond felt a wave of self-centered remorse. His purpose for coming here was to find and observe creatures like these, as well as every other living thing he encountered. It had been a last-ditch attempt to produce a doctoral dissertation that might gain him some notoriety. Sure, bridging excursions had been the focus of research before, but none of the attempts had amounted to much, due to the limitations of bridging. The researchers simply couldn't remember enough detail to create more than a superficial, descriptive account of their destination worlds. But with Desmond it was different, which was why his supervising professors hadn't rejected his dissertation proposal.

His entire research mission had gone out the window within seconds of bridging to this world. Months of careful planning and a million and a half of Xavier's family money, all wasted. And a good bridger had died trying to protect them. The whole thing was a disaster. Even if they managed to survive until bridge-back, Desmond had little to look forward to upon returning except guilt, shame at his arrogance, and an uncertain future.

The next hill was taller than the first two, and he emerged from the trees onto the summit breathing hard. He turned his back to the river to gaze down at a wide, mostly-treeless valley that spread out into the distance. The sight nearly took his breath away. A herd of hundreds—maybe thousands—of animals grazed near the center. Smaller groups of creatures of another type dotted the valley here and there. At this distance, he couldn't make out details, but he could see that all of them walked on two legs.

The view was truly mesmerizing, but he had been gone too long. He gathered an armload of grass stems and headed back. As he descended the hill, he spotted a patch of the same rigid plants they had used to make sharpened weapons. They had abandoned the last of the weapons when they'd escaped from the shelter, so he took a detour away from the river to get some. For several minutes, he watched a bewildering variety of flies and butterfly-like insects swarming around the green bubble structures at the tip of each stalk. Finally he sighed and pulled up four of the stalks.

He angled back toward the river. He was applying yet another layer of mud after re-crossing the small stream, when he heard something approaching. The rustling of dead bubble leaves, a splash in the stream, and then the crack of a fairly large branch—unmistakable sounds of a heavy creature. It was close, but he couldn't see it yet. Which meant it couldn't see him. He carefully stepped to a cluster of small trees and stood behind them, watching.

There was movement at about fifty yards up the stream, glimpses of dark brown. Seconds later it came into full view—the same type of monstrous predator that had killed and eaten Razor. The creature was walking along the stream. It was already too close for Desmond to creep away without being seen. It was coming directly toward him—he would have to run. The thing was massive, but there was no doubt it could outrun him. With paralyzing clarity, Desmond realized he was screwed.

He willed himself to run, but he was frozen in place. If he ran, his life would probably end within seconds. If he stayed there, maybe there was a chance the creature would change direction.

It kept coming.

Abruptly, the thing stopped. It raised its beak as if sniffing the air. It looked to one side and then the other, still sniffing. Desmond's heart was racing, and his hands were starting to shake. He closed his eyes, trying to relax, to control his movements the way Infinity had instructed.

When he opened his eyes, the creature was looking directly at him. Desmond didn't dare blink. Instead, he slowly closed his eyelids until he was looking through narrow slits, hoping to keep his eyes moist enough to avoid the need to blink. The predator stared, not moving a muscle. Excruciating seconds passed. Desmond knew the thing was unlikely to simply turn around and go away. If he wanted to live, he would have to run—maybe get up into a tree before the creature caught him. But still, his legs refused.

Finally, the creature took a step. It then crouched low to the ground.

Desmond turned and ran. Immediately he heard the predator take off in pursuit, crashing through everything in its path. Several trees with low branches whisked by Desmond, but the predator was too close behind for him to try to climb. The only thing he could think of was to run straight for the river, jump in, and try to make it across. But he still couldn't see the water, and the creature was gaining on him.

He ran past something that caught his eye—something that seemed out of place. Confused, he snapped his head back to look. It was a dead, mangled animal, skewered against a huge tree by two sharpened poles at the chest height.

The predator stopped pursuing him. Desmond's momentum took him a few more steps, but he came to a stop and stared back, trying to comprehend what was happening. The predator sniffed the air. It then stepped up to the dead animal and stared at it.

Desmond was only thirty yards ahead. He should have been running, but something about the situation kept him in place. Before he could ask himself what it was, the huge predator lunged forward, clamped its beak onto the dead animal, and shook it. At the same moment, something exploded from the branches above, scattering bubble-leaves and slamming down onto the predator. It was so sudden and violent that Desmond stumbled back and fell on his butt.

He got to his feet and stepped closer. The predator was dead, pinned to the ground by rows of sharpened poles that had pushed all the way through its body. The poles were attached to a rectangular frame by tightly-wrapped cord. Tied atop the frame were several large stones, obviously there to provide additional momentum.

Desmond realized he wasn't breathing and sucked in a lungful of air. He suddenly felt helpless and exposed. Something—or someone—had set a trap.

As stealthily as he could, Desmond returned to where he'd first seen the predator and retrieved the bundle of grass and the rigid stalks. These materials were more important now than he had previously realized. He made his way to the top of the first hill and grabbed the other bundle of grass. He descended that hill and made his way up to the summit of the cliff face. He found the others hunkered down in a low area where they were less visible. Panting from the climb, he dumped the materials beside them and joined them on the ground.

"We're not alone," he said.

Lenny and Xavier stared at him.

"Clarify," Infinity said.

"There's an intelligent species here. At least intelligent enough to construct a highly effective kill trap for large animals."

Infinity sat up straight and swiveled her head, looking in every direction. "Describe the kill trap. Did it have any parts that indicate an industrial or technological society, like metal or plastic?"

He shook his head. "Nothing like that. Wood mostly, tied together with cord. Rocks tied on for weight."

She mouthed a silent curse. "Just what we need." She then seemed to realize they were waiting for her to explain. "Primitive non-human tribes are bad news. At least in my experience."

"Maybe they'd be willing to help us," Lenny said. "It'd be freaking mind-blowing to meet them."

Infinity shook her head. "Not an option."

Lenny persisted. "How can you know that? Don't be so pessimistic about people. It's all in how you present yourself to them. I think they might help us."

"We don't even know what they are," Desmond said. "They can't possibly be human. Not even close to human. It's been eighty million years since this universe diverged from ours. We haven't seen a single mammal. I'm willing to bet there *are* no mammals. Think about it—this world was the same as ours until eighty million years ago. So the dinosaurs, pterosaurs, insects, therapsids, mammals, and everything else were identical to ours at that point. And they probably continued to be somewhat similar after the divergence point, at least for another fourteen million years until the Chicxulub asteroid caused the KT extinction. I suppose it's possible the asteroid didn't even strike in this universe, but most likely it did."

"It almost certainly did," Xavier said. "The damn thing was six miles across. There aren't a lot of random things that could happen in only fourteen million years that could change its course."

Desmond said, "So we'll assume the asteroid struck this world. In which case the KT extinction took place here. But what's interesting—and it's the reason I wanted a world with divergence at eighty million years—is that, as we all know, the KT extinction caused an evolutionary bottleneck. As many as 75% of the existing species were wiped out. On our world, the small mammals that existed at that time thrived and diversified. And although the non-avian dinosaurs became extinct, the avian dinosaurs thrived and diversified into thousands of species of birds. The—"

A disturbing shriek erupted from somewhere in the forest near the river below. It sounded like one animal being killed by another. After a few seconds it stopped abruptly.

Infinity shoved the pile of grasses and several rocks at Desmond, Xavier, and Lenny. "We need rope. If you have to talk, do it while making cords."

Desmond, Xavier, and Lenny began twisting and wrapping while Infinity sharpened the ends of the four stalks Desmond had brought.

Vocalizing his thoughts was helping Desmond keep his mind off the fact that they could be attacked at any moment, so he continued. "The diversification of life after the KT extinction could just as easily have gone any number of other ways. There was no guarantee that mammals would thrive. That's the thing about evolutionary bottlenecks—small random events can make a huge difference. We see it over and over again in our own world, when a small population of living things becomes isolated. The Galapagos islands, for example. Anyway, after the KT extinction, almost anything could have happened."

"And based on what we've seen here," Xavier said, "the avian dinosaurs that survived the extinction event got the upper hand. They diversified and filled all the niches the mammals otherwise would have."

"Exactly," Desmond said.

Lenny grunted. "So they're not human. Doesn't flipping matter. If they're intelligent, they're probably basically compassionate."

Xavier said, "You're absurdly naive, Lenny. And in case you haven't noticed, you and I are crippled. If you happen to be wrong, we can't even run away."

"Which is why we need the rope," Infinity said. "Less talking, more twisting."

THE FINISHED ROPE was surprisingly strong, as Infinity had promised. It was only an inch in diameter, but their tests had proven it would hold Lenny's weight, and Lenny was the heaviest.

Still, the thought of hanging from it over a 50-foot cliff made Desmond feel ill. Apparently Xavier and Lenny were feeling the same way, because they had become somber once they realized it was time to actually use the rope.

Infinity, of course, was not interested in wasting time. She stepped to the edge of the bluff and dangled the rope. "Lenny, you're first. There isn't enough to tie around you. Just grip it above the knot." She pulled the rope back up and held the end of it out to him. "Are you strong enough for this?"

He took the rope. "My foot's mangled, not my hands."

Desmond felt the need to address the obvious problem. "The rope's barely long enough, and there's nothing to tie it to anyway. How's the last person going to get down?"

Infinity said, "I'm the last. Once the three of you are safe, I'll make more rope."

Desmond looked around. "There's nothing here to tie it to."

Her mud-crusted eyes narrowed. "I'll figure it out. We're wasting time, tourist." She took the rope, sat on the edge of the cliff, and braced her feet against a crack in the rock surface. "Sit behind me," she said to Desmond.

He sighed and sat down.

"Closer," she said. "We don't have any rope to spare."

He inched forward until he was pressed against her back, his legs on either side of her thighs.

"Xavier, you're behind Desmond."

Xavier grunted in pain as he scooted into place. Infinity passed the rope back and they all gripped it on their right.

Infinity spoke to Lenny. "Lay on your belly and go over the edge feet-first. Then just hold on, and we'll do the rest."

Lenny moved into place, and they began lowering him down a few inches at a time, which was surprisingly easy. Desmond felt the rope stretch and tighten down on itself, just as Infinity had said it would. Lenny remained silent as he descended.

"I've got the knot in my hand," Xavier said, his voice strained. "There's no more."

"Don't let go," Infinity instructed, "but extend your arm past Desmond."

Xavier slid forward until he was pressed against Desmond's back. Desmond half-expected him to make a joke about it, but Xavier only grunted in his ear.

Suddenly the weight on the rope was gone.

"I'm in!" Lenny called out from below. "It's big enough for all of us."

Infinity leaned over the edge and spoke in a low tone. "Do not shout. Understand?"

"Sorry. Uh, there's a lot of bird shit in here. A *lot*."

She ignored him and got back into position. "You're up, Xavier. Are you strong enough to hold your own weight?"

"I'm exhausted and probably in shock. Do I have a choice?"

"If you're too weak, you'll wait up here with me until we can create a harness. My priority is to get you safely into the cave."

He sighed and gingerly touched his lower leg. Desmond was glad the leg was covered in mud. When they had crossed the river, the mud had been washed away, revealing stomach-churning bruising from the knee down.

Xavier said, "I guess I'd rather die from falling than from being eaten."

She frowned at him. "Again, can you hold your weight?"

He nodded. "I can do it, don't worry."

Desmond and Infinity lowered him over the edge. About a minute later Xavier cried out in pain, and the rope went slack.

"He's okay," Lenny called up in a hushed voice.

Infinity repositioned her feet for better leverage. "Let's get this done," she said.

Desmond considered her plan for a moment, and then he stood up. "I'm staying up here."

She looked up at him. "No you're not."

"I'll help you make more rope. Then we'll figure out how to tie it off, and we'll both go down."

She got to her feet and faced him. "Like I said, my priority is getting you into the cave where it's safe."

"Well, if I help you, then it will take less time before *you're* there in the cave to protect us. Besides, once I'm in that hole in the rock, my observations will be limited. I came here to collect information."

Her gaze was intense, and the mud caked on her face made it seem even more intimidating. "The moment we bridged and your friend broke his leg, this excursion was no longer about you collecting information." She took a step toward him.

He held his hands up as if surrendering, although he had no intention of changing his mind. "I understand that. But you and Razor saved our lives. I'm not leaving you alone up here while all three of us sit in that hole."

She glared at him for several more seconds. "Suit yourself, tourist."

"I'm not trying to make your job harder, I just—"

He was interrupted by a shrill whistle. They both turned and looked down the hillside to the tree line.

A group of creatures had emerged from the trees. Several of them had stopped and were staring up at the humans. The one in the lead made another whistling sound, and they all stopped, at least a dozen of them.

Desmond stared, his throat tightening. The bird-like creatures had the same basic body plan as the other large animals they'd seen —two legs, small arms, a coat of fine hair or feathers, and a beak. But there was one glaring difference. Each of these creatures was laden with tools or weapons. They gripped short spears in their hands. Thick coils of rope hung from the necks of some of them, while others bore strange devices that could have been some kind of crossbow.

"Our plans just changed again," Infinity muttered.

8

CONTACT

Infinity cursed silently. She should have forced the tourist to get into to the cave. She should have put him out with a chokehold, tied the rope to his feet, and pushed him over the side. The creatures now watching them from farther down the slope were bad news. She had known that after taking one look at them.

"Stay calm," she said softly to Desmond. "Do nothing that appears aggressive. We have to lead them away from the cave and hope they don't already know your friends are there."

The tourist suddenly shouted. "Lenny and Xavier, do not acknowledge that you hear me. We have company, and we don't want them to know where you are. Stay quiet."

A barely-audible "Oh shit!" came from below.

Infinity glared at Desmond, although she realized he'd done the right thing.

The creatures on the hillside looked at each other and began talking. Or at least it seemed like talking. They went back and forth with rapid whistles, squawks, chuckles, and clicks. Most likely, they were surprised and confused. This confusion was good, but only if she and Desmond acted immediately.

"We're going to start by slowly leading them away," she said to Desmond. "They're going to follow us, whether they're aggressive or just curious. We'll walk straight away from the river to divert them from the cave." She picked up the four sharpened stalks. This act might have appeared aggressive, but she wasn't going anywhere without them.

They began walking. The creatures followed, as expected, angling toward them and still chittering at each other like a flock of 100-pound parrots. They descended the hill as it gently sloped away from the river. The rocky hillside offered no cover, and the tree line was several hundred yards away.

She cursed herself again for not making the tourist get in the cave.

He was starting to get ahead of her, glancing over his shoulder like he might run at any second.

"Slower! Show confidence."

He slowed his pace. "Easier said than done. Besides, they can't know what human confidence looks like."

Still talking to each other, the creatures began spreading out. Infinity gauged the distance to the trees again. The bird men were walking faster now, and she could see that they would surround her and Desmond before they could reach the tree line. This was bad. The creatures needed to be lured farther from Lenny and Xavier. Even if she couldn't save Desmond, at least the other two would be safe until bridge-back.

"We're going to run," she said.

"Are you sure that's wise?"

She looked at Desmond's feet. They were bleeding, which made his running ability unpredictable. "Follow me. Keep up and do *not* get separated." She took one more look at the approaching bird men. They were continuing to spread out. The time was now.

"Now!" She took off for the tree line with the tourist right behind her.

The creatures' chattering erupted into ear-splitting squawks. Infinity glanced over her shoulder. As expected, the bird men were now running. She glanced again and saw that they were quickly catching up. She and Desmond would make it into the trees before being overtaken, but not much beyond that. Several plans ran through her mind, none of them pleasant. The plan she chose would depend on the creatures' behavior and the terrain once they reached the forest.

They broke through the brushy tree line. The forest floor was uneven and cluttered. Fallen trees and low vegetation would make all-out running impossible. Infinity looked back at their pursuers. The creatures were no longer spreading out. Instead, they were funneling into the forest at the spot where the humans had entered. Only one of her plans would work in this situation. But first they would need more of a lead.

"Faster!" she said. She jumped over logs and plowed through thick vegetation.

"I'm trying!"

Ahead was a particularly thick jumble of brush growing in and around a fallen tree. It would have to do. She headed straight for it. Ten yards out she turned to the tourist and said, "In a moment you're going to do what I say. No questions."

He was panting and starting to limp. "Okay."

They rounded the side of the brushy tangle, and she put on the brakes, sliding to a stop on her side. "Get down!"

The tourist skidded awkwardly to the ground beside her.

She pushed him toward the pile. "Get inside. I'm right behind you."

He crawled into the brush. "I'm in. Come on—there's room for both of us."

She tossed three of the sharpened stalks in after him and kept the other. "If you move one muscle, you die. Stay here!" She got up and ran before he had a chance to protest. She angled away from the pursuing creatures. As she ran, she began talking loudly between gasps for air. "If you'd gone... to the goddamn cave... like I told you to... I wouldn't be trying... this stupid plan... to draw these... butt-ugly birds... away from you."

She paused and turned to the creatures. It looked like the entire flock had angled toward her, following her voice, which was what she had hoped for. She started running again and poured on the speed, ducking, dodging, and jumping. All she had to do now was lose them and then return for the obstinate tourist and take him to the cave. And this time he was getting in, even if she had to render him unconscious.

But the creatures were gaining on her. She couldn't run any faster over this terrain. She weighed possible plans again. They were still too close to the tourist for her to stop and hide, fight, or surrender. If the creatures had any brains at all, they'd search the area and find him. This left few choices—her first priority was to lure them farther from the tourist.

She stumbled and nearly fell as she pounded through a low muddy spot, but she quickly recovered and headed up the next hill. She ducked behind a large tree at the top of the hill and looked back. The creatures converged on the low area and came to a stop. They were looking at the ground rather than up at her, which meant they had lost her. One of them pointed at the mud with its tiny hand. The others looked at the spot. It was exactly where she had passed—they had found her tracks. At once they all looked up the hill, directly at her.

She cursed and took off again. She ran to the crest of the hill and across the open grassy summit. Suddenly she was out of space. Before her was a dizzying drop to the river. She had thought the river was far to her left, but apparently a large bend brought it around into a U shape.

She heard the creatures running up the hill. They were seconds from coming into view. On the ground to her left was a jagged notch in the crest of the cliff. She darted over to it. It turned out to be more than a notch—it was a deep crevice, disappearing into darkness. She threw herself onto the rock surface and slid into the crevice, thrusting out her hands and knees to keep from slipping too far down and getting wedged in. The jagged edge of the rock cut into her skin, and her sharpened weapon fell from her hand, tumbling out of sight.

A whistle came from above, followed by cackling and clicking. The creatures had arrived. If they came near the crevice, they would definitely see her. She slid down the rock a few more inches, scraping her palms and knees. She barely stopped herself from grunting aloud from the pain. She couldn't stay in this tortuous position for long. She looked around. Her eyes had adjusted somewhat to the darkness, and now she noticed an even darker area a few yards to her left, near where the crevice opened to the space above the river. It was a cavity where a large chunk of rock had fallen out—a possible hiding spot.

The bird-like chattering above got louder as more of the creatures arrived. As silently as possible, she inched her way toward the cavity, scraping skin from her knees and back. She reached the edge of the cavity and pushed herself into it. It was shallow, but it might work as a hiding spot as long as the creatures didn't stare down into the crevice for too long.

The chattering seemed to draw nearer. Something above cast a shadow over the crevice and hovered there. Infinity glanced up and saw that one of the creatures was peeking over the edge, looking down. She held her breath, shrinking back into the cavity as much as possible. A few seconds later the shadow pulled back and was gone.

Unable to do anything else, she listened to the creatures cackling. It was so frantic and complex she couldn't imagine how they understood each other. Gradually, some of the voices drifted away. More shadows passed by as several of the creatures leapt over the crevice. If they were to look down from the other side, the angle might give them a better view into the cavity. But they continued on their way. A minute or so later only a few voices remained, and then it was silent.

Their scattering suggested they had split up and were still looking for her. The area wouldn't be safe until they had given up. Since they weren't even close to being human, it was impossible to guess how long that would take. She tried to maneuver into a more comfortable position and eventually gave up. There was nothing to do but wait. As long as the tourist had stayed where she'd left him, there was still a good chance of getting him to the safety of the cave with the other two. Assuming the bird creatures hadn't already found the cave.

Minutes passed. She tried counting seconds but grew weary of it after three hundred.

A shadow moved over the crevice. She glanced up. One of the creatures stood on the opposite side of the crevice's mouth, staring down. She could see its eyes, which probably meant it could see her. Suddenly she realized how helpless she was in this hiding spot. Climbing out would make her vulnerable, and she wouldn't be able to fight until she climbed out.

The creature turned its head, looking from one end of the crevice to the other. Abruptly, it lowered its head to look closer. It was staring right at her. For several seconds it didn't move. Then it threw its head back and let out a high whistle, no doubt alerting the others.

In a distinctly non-human motion, it used its forearms to pull something hanging from its neck up and over its head. The object looked like some kind of slingshot or crossbow, and Infinity realized she needed to act quickly.

She held her hands out and spoke softly. "I'm not here to hurt you. Please don't hurt me."

It paused and gazed at her. It then held the device out with both hands as if offering it to her. But Infinity knew better. She could see that the device had a fletched arrow resting in the flight groove of a center shaft pointed directly at her. The creature grabbed the fletched end of the arrow with its beak and pulled back, bending the tension limbs that protruded from each side.

Infinity shrank back into the cavity as far as she could. "Don't do it, shit-bird!"

She heard a snap and felt a burning in her hip. She threw her hand over the spot. The arrow had passed almost all the way through the flesh of her right hip. She moved her hand to the exit wound, where the arrow was protruding. The arrow jiggled easily, which meant it wasn't lodged in her hip bone.

She looked up at the creature, furious. It removed another arrow from beneath the weapon's center shaft and began putting it into place. She screamed with rage, pulled the arrow the rest of the way out, and launched herself upward, lodging her body against both rock surfaces above the cavity. She ignored the pain and began frantically working her way up, focusing all of her thoughts on killing the creature with her bare hands.

But it was taking her too long. The creature had gotten the arrow in place and was holding the weapon out with both hands, clamping its beak onto the bowstring.

Infinity, still several feet below the crevice opening, realized she was going to take another hit, and this one would be much worse.

The bird pulled back, aiming at her, ready to release the arrow.

"No!" she cried, tucking her head below her arms to avoid being shot in the face.

She heard a dull thud, and then a heavy weight crashed onto her head and shoulders, knocking her several excruciating feet back down into the crevice. The heavy object rolled off her and became

wedged into the tighter space below. It began grunting and struggling, but it had little room to move. It was the bird creature.

"Grab hold!"

She looked up. Desmond was kneeling above her, extending
one of the crude spears down for her to grab.

9

MUD

Desmond waited, holding his sharpened stalk out for Infinity to grab. She didn't look so good. Her eyes were wide, the first time he had seen her display any hint of fear. Her blood was smeared on the rock faces on either side of her, and more blood was dripping from her thigh onto the creature wedged into the crevice below. The thing was barely struggling to free itself, obviously dazed. Desmond had hit it upside the head as hard as he could with his stalk.

"You should hurry," he said.

She grunted and grabbed the stalk while using her legs to keep herself from falling deeper. Desmond leaned back, straining to pull her up. She scaled the edge and sprawled on her face on the rock surface beside him. Blood was still dripping from her hip, already forming a puddle.

"That looks bad," he said, pressing his hand against the hole on the back of her hip to stop the flow. He then realized blood was also flowing from the front of her hip. "Jesus, it went all the way though."

She got to her feet, grimacing in pain. "We have to go. The others are coming." She took a step and stumbled.

Desmond put her left arm over his shoulder, and she didn't protest the help. They headed for the nearest tree line. At ten yards from the forest, one of the bird people emerged from the brush directly in front of them. The thing saw them and stopped, apparently surprised.

"Maybe this one will be friendly," Desmond whispered.

The creature whistled loudly and reached for the crossbow hanging from its neck.

In a flash, Infinity grabbed Desmond's spear from his hand, hefted herself from his shoulder, and closed the distance to the creature with startling speed. At the last second, she used her good leg to launch herself into the air, spun completely around, and kicked the startled creature in the neck. The creature crumpled to the ground. Infinity landed on one foot, still spinning, and raised the sharpened stalk above her head as she completed the second circle. She grunted and drove it through the creature where its neck joined its body. The thing started flailing around, so she pulled the spear out and stabbed again and again until it was still.

She stood above the bird man with her eyes closed, taking slow, deep breaths to cope with the pain she had inflicted upon herself. A few seconds later, she opened her eyes and held her arm out toward Desmond. "Let's go."

Desmond stared at her for a moment, trying to process what had just happened. He snapped out of it and rushed to her side. She put her arm over his shoulder again, and together they pushed their way through the brush and into the forest.

A whistle came from somewhere to their left. It was answered by another straight ahead. Infinity pointed to the right, and they headed that direction. As they moved through the forest, Desmond noticed out of the corner of his vision that Infinity kept glancing at the trees above.

"Wait," she whispered. When they had come to a stop, she nodded upward. "There."

He looked. "More climbing?"

"We have no choice."

He helped her to the base of the tree, which she'd apparently chosen for its immense height and accessible branches. He waited for Infinity to start climbing first and then followed her up. He heard her whimpering softly each time she pulled herself higher.

Desmond said, "They'll be pissed when they see what we've done to two of their companions."

She paused and looked down at him with a finger pressed to her lips.

They continued climbing until they came upon two thick limbs growing side-by-side from the main trunk, one slightly higher than the other. Infinity straddled one of the limbs with her back to the trunk, and Desmond sat on the other limb. They were a good fifty feet above the ground, with enough branches and bubble leaves below to provide at least some concealment.

Infinity pulled her legs up and rested them in front of her on her limb. She tapped Desmond and nodded at her legs. He lifted his own legs onto his limb, although he had to cross them to prevent them from sliding back off. The strangely-soft covering of the trunk and limb almost felt like skin against his body.

They waited.

Over the next several minutes a few whistles came from different directions. Desmond glimpsed one of the creatures walking below, making its way back to the rocky summit of the hill. It would likely find the bird man Infinity had killed at the edge of the forest, as well as the injured one in the crevice at the summit.

Things were quiet for several more minutes. But then they heard a cacophony of squawks and whistles in the distance as the bird creatures gathered. No doubt they would intensify their search.

He turned to Infinity. To stop her blood from dripping, she was pressing one hand to the wound on the front of her hip while pressing her other hand to the wound in the back.

She noticed he was staring at her. "I told you to stay where I left you," she hissed.

He raised his brows, cracking the last of the mud still coating his forehead. "You're welcome."

She exhaled and pressed her head against the trunk behind her, trying to ignore the pain. But she managed a nod. "Thank you."

"We have to stop the bleeding," he said.

She nodded again. "I need to climb to the ground. To get what I need."

"I'll go get what you need."

She gazed at him, thinking. "Sunset is close. An hour, maybe. Our best option is to stay here. But I won't last if I can't plug this up." She quietly listened for a moment. "They're still talking. I agree—you should go." She glanced at her hip and sighed. "I'm a liability now."

"Just tell me what you need."

"A handful of pliable mud. And several fresh, flat leaves, each at least three inches across. From a tree, not from the ground."

Desmond looked at the bubble leaves around them. Several were within reach, so he plucked one off. Like all the others, it was green-tinted and full of air. He popped it with his fingers and then tore it in half. He held up the two halves.

She nodded. "Should work."

He looked down, surveying the area below. "Okay, I'll be back as quickly as possible." He slid his legs off the limb and started climbing down.

She grabbed his arm. "Follow the slope. There's a stream at the bottom. Don't move fast—move smart. The only sure defense is to not be seen."

He nodded. "I won't be long." He descended from the tree,

thinking about Infinity's condition. He was worried—she wouldn't have allowed him to do this if it weren't absolutely necessary.

Once on the ground, Desmond realized he could no longer hear the bird creatures talking, either due to his lower position or because they had separated to renew their search. He crept down the slope to the stream, watching and listening for any movement. After quickly refreshing the layer of mud on his body, he used both hands to gather what he could carry. Several minutes later he arrived back at the tree, apparently undetected. He pressed the lump of mud to his belly and tried climbing with his other hand. This wasn't working, so he had to take what mud he could in one fist, looping that arm over limbs when needed. Several drops of Infinity's blood hit his face as he climbed.

When he was halfway up, a noisy chittering sound erupted from above and to his left, startling him. At first he didn't see it, but then it moved—a small black animal with a pale gray belly. It could only be described as a squirrel with a beak and feathers. And it was angry.

Desmond looked down uncomfortably, aware that the noise the squirrel was making could alert the bird men. He waved his arm at it and spoke in a whisper. "Get!"

The squirrel stopped. A few seconds later it started again. Desmond tried shaking a limb, having no effect. Finally, he resorted to throwing a chunk of the mud he'd collected. This sent the creature scampering away, and it jumped to another tree and disappeared. Again he checked the area below for signs of their pursuers and then continued climbing.

Finally, he positioned himself beside Infinity. "This is all I've got."

"It's enough. Hold it out right there." She pressed one of the halves of the bubble leaf over the hole in her hip. Holding it in place with one hand, she grabbed half the mud with her other hand and placed it on the leaf. "Hold my arm. Don't let me fall."

Desmond didn't like the sound of this, but he turned and gripped her arm below the shoulder with his free hand.

"Watch what I do," she said. She pushed her finger two inches into the wound, forcing mud into it, the leaf folding up around the mud as a sheath. Her head slammed back against the soft bark of the tree as she stifled a cry. Desmond held her steady. She looked back down at her hip, pulled her finger out, and stuffed more of the mud into the hole until it was full. She then closed her eyes, taking deep breaths.

"You okay?"

She handed him the other half of the leaf. "You need to do the exit wound." She then leaned to the side, turning her right butt cheek toward him, and gripped a limb that was above her head.

"You're not serious. I can't do that."

"Don't be a pussy, Decay."

He looked at the wound. Blood was still dripping out, and the layer of mud on the skin around it was stained red and smeared into messy patterns. "Why do you need the mud? Can't I just push the leaf in there?"

"The mud makes a good plug. Shove it in so it expands below the wound opening. When it's wider than the opening, it won't fall out. Please, Desmond, just get it done."

"Well, if you're resorting to using my real name... hold on." He put some mud on the leaf and jammed it into the hole.

She bucked and stifled another cry.

He then packed in more mud until he was sure it was wider than the hole. "Finished."

She eased back to her sitting position and rested there with her eyes closed. Finally, she said, "Thirty-six hours can be a long time."

He huffed out a quiet laugh and then stared out at what was now obviously the western sky. "Well, at least we have good seats for the sunset." The clouds above the horizon glowed with a shade of red not quite like any sunset he had ever seen on his own world. Or maybe that was just his imagination.

She opened her eyes and stared at the sky. "No humans have ever seen the sun set on this world."

"I imagine you've had a lot of opportunities to say that."

"Not really. Most tourists aren't crazy enough to bridge to a world with an eighty-million-year divergence."

For several minutes they watched in silence as the sun dropped behind the other treetops. Desmond suddenly realized the temperature had dropped at least ten degrees. When the sun was no longer visible, the relatively silent forest seemed to wake up. Countless insects, and probably other creatures Desmond couldn't even imagine, began calling. It was a living symphony of sounds completely alien to human ears.

By the time Desmond spoke again, he had to raise his voice above a whisper in order to be heard. "It's going to be a long night. I don't think I'll be able to sleep without falling."

She didn't answer.

"I keep seeing the way you killed that bird man in my head," he said. "Where did you learn to kick like that?"

"I learned it before I was ten. It's a 540 kick. Because you spin 540 degrees. I figured it was a move a stupid bird wouldn't expect."

"So you've always been a fighter?"

She waited a few seconds before answering. "Before I was seventeen, I fought because I had to. After that I fought for money."

"Your online profile said you were a mixed martial arts fighter."

"Mostly. After high school I tried making a living at it. Six years. Something I don't recommend. Then a rep from SafeTrek came to my training club and gave a spiel. They were looking for good hand-to-hand fighters. Because weapons don't bridge. Adventure and good pay for the right person. So I applied."

"Doyle told us you're the best bridger he's ever seen."

She blew out a brief laugh. "Only because I haven't died yet."

Desmond wasn't sure how to respond to that, so he stared at the sky. The first stars were showing up. He knew the stars would be pretty much identical to those he'd see if he were back in his own universe. Not much could happen to stars in only eighty million years.

"Your turn," she said, just loud enough to be heard over the night creatures. "Tell me about yourself."

"What do you want to know?"

"Nothing really. I just figured it was your turn."

He turned and stared at her in the fading light. She may have been smiling slightly, but he couldn't tell for sure. "I can tell you this," he said. "I don't want to die here, but I'm not excited about going back."

She shifted her head slightly to gaze at him. "Not what I expected."

"Well, I'm going to have almost nothing to show for this excursion. I had carefully planned an entire sequence of observations, focusing on the types of data I'm good at recalling. That all went out the window seconds after we arrived. Other than random things I've encountered, I won't have much of anything for my dissertation. They've already given me too many extensions and free passes. Three years in my PhD program, and now I'll never finish. I think I was in over my head from the beginning anyway."

"I thought you had a photographic memory."

"Recalling information isn't everything."

"Why did you leave your hiding spot and follow me?" she asked, changing the subject.

"The bird men were chasing you. I waited until they had all passed by. I thought you might need help. Turns out I was right." He watched her, but she didn't respond. He noticed she was shivering. He said, "The temperature has dropped more than I thought it would. I'm afraid it's going to get pretty cold by morning."

"The air here is dry, that's why."

"You're cold already."

She nodded. "It's the blood loss."

He looked down at the two limbs supporting them. Hers was wider than his. "Um, I'm not trying to be a creep, but maybe we should—"

"Yes, we can save heat by reducing surface area. And you're not being a creep—you're being smart. My body needs rest or I'll be worthless to you tomorrow." She inched forward on her limb, leaving a gap between her back and the trunk. "Sit behind me."

At this moment it seemed anything he could say would be awkward, so he silently got up and maneuvered into place behind her. After a bit of fumbling, he was able to place his feet on the limb with his knees bent outward and her legs resting on top of his feet. It was reasonably comfortable. He put one arm around her waist. With his other hand he gripped the same limb she'd clung to when he had plugged her wound.

They sat this way for several minutes without talking. It felt surprisingly comforting having her warm body against his.

Suddenly she gripped his leg so hard it hurt.

He was about to protest when he heard it, too—a creature moving on the forest floor below. He glanced down, but the space below was an ocean of blackness. Each step the creature took produced a low thud on the soil. It was large, much larger than the bird men. It stopped every few steps, and he could hear it sniffing the air. It must have tracked their scent to this tree. It began walking back the way it had come but then doubled back and stopped beneath them again. Could a creature that large climb the tree? It walked back and forth several more times, and then it wandered off, its footsteps slowly growing fainter and fading away.

Desmond let out a long breath. "I can't imagine putting myself in situations like this for a living. But I bet you've seen some amazing things."

She leaned her bald head back to rest on his chest. "You don't see things the way I do. You see things that amaze you. I see only threats."

He considered this. He suddenly had a new understanding of the vast differences between her life and his. She had grown up fighting, probably for her very life. Then she had continued fighting to survive, but in a different way—to make money. And now she was fighting to save the lives of tourists.

"Do you enjoy what you do? Being a bridger, I mean."

"Not today."

He decided to change the subject. "Infinity is a good bridger name. But I wouldn't mind knowing your real name."

"We don't tell tourists our real names."

"Well, this tourist saved your life today. Don't I deserve a little more?"

Her shoulders shook once, perhaps a brief chuckle. "Maybe you do. My name's Passerina."

He had heard that name before. Suddenly he made the connection. "The painted bunting!" He moved his hand from her belly and put his finger on the tattoo on her chest. "That explains the tattoo."

She didn't respond to this, so he moved his hand back to her waist. He would have to hold on to her all night to keep her from falling if she fell asleep.

After a few minutes of silence, he said. "It's cool that your parents named you after a bird."

She didn't respond to this.

"It's also cool that you keep having the tattoo re-inked."

Still she didn't respond.

He sighed. Maybe she just didn't feel like talking. Then he noticed her breathing had become rhythmic. She was already asleep.

Desmond looked up at the stars. He tightened his grip on the limb he'd been using for stability and tightened his other arm around Infinity.

10

PETS

August 4

INFINITY'S EYES FLICKED OPEN. Her surroundings had changed. Instead of darkness and stars she saw blue sky and bubble leaves. She wasn't sure it was real. She had awakened so many times, each time struggling to differentiate between reality and disturbing dreams about Razor being attacked again and again by beaked predators. Something tightened around her waist. A warm arm.

"You really awake this time?" The voice was inches from her ear.

"I think so. Yes. Shit. I can't believe I fell asleep."

"You needed rest."

"I suppose you stayed awake all night. Otherwise I would've fallen, and I'd be busted up on the ground."

"Yeah. It's a good thing I'm dehydrated. Taking a pee would have been awkward." Desmond shifted his weight to the side, and hazy memories came back to Infinity of him doing that over and over during the night.

She pulled his arm from her waist and sat up straight. Her hip burned as she shifted, and she sensed that it would have been much worse if she hadn't slept. "You've saved my life twice now," she said.

"A couple more times and we'll be even."

She inspected her hip wound. It looked infected as hell, but it wasn't bleeding. The plugs were doing their job. If she made it to bridge-back, they'd bombard her with antibiotics, give her a few weeks off, and then assign her to another excursion. She leaned back against the warmth of Desmond's body. "It's August. Why is it so cold?" She pulled his arm around her waist again, which helped.

He shifted again. "Like you said last night, the air here is dry, maybe because these trees don't transpire like ours do. And there are countless other changes that could have occurred in the last eighty million years."

She began weighing the merits of several courses of action. Based on the sun's height above the eastern horizon, bridge-back was probably twelve hours away. Maybe the safest option was to stay where they were.

"We need to get back to Lenny and Xavier," the tourist said, as if he had sensed what she was thinking. "They may need our help."

"They'll be safe until bridge-back. If the damn bird men are still crawling all over this area, the last thing we want to do is reveal your friends' location by attempting to go there." She was glad they were contained where they couldn't get out. It gave her one less thing to worry about. But she decided not to share this with Desmond.

"Maybe you're right. But I wish we could at least check on them—see if they made it through the night okay."

She decided she'd better get his mind off that idea before he started dwelling on it. "Tell me about how you managed to arrange this excursion. Most tourists either pay for it with some kind of research grant or they're filthy-rich adrenaline junkies. The three of you seem different."

"I share an apartment with Lenny and Xavier back in Columbia—South Carolina, not the country. We're all in biology degree programs at USC, so we have that in common. We were drinking one night, and Lenny suggested this idea for my dissertation. I knew it was crazy, but later I couldn't stop thinking about it. And things gradually fell into place. Xavier liked the idea and wanted to come, which was fortunate because his family owns a chain of New York bookstores called Middle Earth Books. Have you heard of them?"

She shook her head. She was already losing interest in his story, but at least he was thinking of other things now.

"So Xavier approached his dad about—"

Infinity grabbed his leg to shut him up. She had seen movement below.

"What?" he whispered.

She pointed, slowly. Something was coming. As it drew nearer, she saw that it was one of the bird men. A smaller two-legged creature walked just ahead of it, straining against a rope leash. It was leading the bird man directly to their tree.

The tourist whispered in her ear. "You've got to be kidding. They have pets?"

The pair stopped directly below, and the smaller one sniffed at the base of the tree. The bird man gazed up, trying to spot them.

A chittering rattle suddenly erupted above the humans' heads. Infinity glanced up. The same damn feathered squirrel from the previous day clung to a limb a few yards above, scolding them with an alarmingly loud call. Perfect.

Desmond waved his arm at the creature, trying to shoo it away.

A shrill whistle came from below. The bird man had spotted them and was calling to the others. It whistled again, even louder.

"What do we do now?" the tourist hissed.

There was only one clear choice. "Climb down!" she said, rolling to the side and clutching another limb. "I'll take this one out. We'll run before the others get here." She twisted sideways, and the fire in her hip nearly caused her to fall. She gritted her teeth and tried to ignore the pain. She started climbing down.

The bird man whistled again and again, aware of what they were trying to do. Infinity assumed it was also preparing its weapon, but she was too busy negotiating the tree limbs to keep an eye on it.

"Infinity, it's too late!"

She paused and looked. Another had arrived, and she glimpsed several more running through the forest. By the time she got to the ground, there would be too many. "Go back up!" she urged as she started climbing. They needed to get out of range of the crossbows.

They climbed until they were at least sixty feet from the ground and could go no higher. At least ten bird men were now standing below, each with its own tracking animal. They stood in a cluster, looking up and chattering to each other. Infinity was pretty sure she and Desmond had climbed beyond the effective range of the primitive crossbows, but the creatures might still try to climb partway up and shoot them. She and the tourist could possibly fight them off if they tried climbing all the way up to drag them down. But not indefinitely. Again, she realized she had chosen a terrible hiding place. Their only hope was to sit tight and try to hold them off until they gave up or until bridge-back. At this point it seemed unlikely they would give up any time soon.

The bird men continued talking for several minutes. Infinity was constantly adjusting her weight, trying to find relief for her hip. Abruptly, the squawks and whistles stopped. The creatures gathered around the base of the tree. Their heads began moving, and Infinity could hear sounds of scratching and crunching.

"What the hell!" the tourist said. "They're chewing on the tree."

He was right. The bird men were biting the tree and tossing aside chunks of the soft, green bark. Infinity watched, not wanting to believe what she was seeing. Within a few minutes, they were through the soft outer layer, and the sounds of their gnawing beaks became louder and more frantic. Based on the size of the chunks they were now tossing aside, progress was slower. But they were still making progress.

She cursed silently and looked around for any possible escape. Other trees were growing near this one, but not near enough to climb from one to the next.

The tourist said, "If we're this high when the tree falls, we'll be killed. Or we'll be knocked to the ground when it hits one of the other trees. We have to move lower. Or we can just surrender."

"Not much of a choice," she said.

"I honestly don't think they're planning to eat us. There are plenty of game animals around, and these guys make excellent traps for them. Why would they go to this much trouble?"

"Doesn't mean they won't kill us."

"Well, we're about to find out."

She sighed and shook her head. After thinking for a few seconds, she said, "Okay, I'm going down. Stay here. Maybe I'll be enough to satisfy them. If so, stay in this tree until bridge-back." She lowered herself painfully to the limb below and began her descent.

The creatures stopped chewing on the tree when they realized what she was doing. With their tracking animals beside them, they stood in a circle, waiting.

Infinity was still considering the possibility of fighting when she stepped to the ground. But when she turned to face the bird men, she realized it would be useless at best and suicide at worst. There were too many of them. And their leashed animals, although smaller than their masters, looked just as formidable.

Despite being fully aware it had done her no good the day

before, she spoke softly. "I'm not here to hurt you. Please don't hurt me."

Several of them held their crossbows in front of them with both hands, ready to pull back the strings with their beaks. Three of them stepped forward, holding out loops of rope, obviously intending to lasso her.

She almost dropped to her knees to allow them to rope her more easily. But then it occurred to her that if she made them work for it, they might decide the tourist wasn't worth the effort.

They stepped closer, readying their ropes. Their round, unblinking eyes darted up and down her body, as if they weren't sure which part of her would prove to be most dangerous.

Infinity looked at the creature approaching on her left and spoke directly to it. "I killed your buddy. I'm going to kill you, too." Then she took a step to the side and threw a roundhouse kick to the bird directly in front of her, catching it off guard. Her foot connected, but the pain in her hip made her double over. Before she could straighten up, the creatures were all over her, and she collapsed under their weight.

Beaks clamped onto her wrists and ankles, but only hard enough to prevent her from flailing. Meaty, prehensile tongues explored her skin, tasting or perhaps feeling her.

"Infinity!"

"Shut up!" she shouted, her face being pressed into the dead leaves and soil. "Stay where you are!"

The creatures deftly tied lengths of rope around her arms and legs, immobilizing her. The bird men then dragged her face down until she was several yards away from the tree. She managed to turn her head to see what they'd do next. They squawked for a few moments, looking up at the tourist. And then, except for two of them that stayed at her side, they went right back to work tearing the trunk apart one bite at a time.

At the edge of her field of vision, Infinity saw the tourist making his way to the ground. The bird men again stopped their assault on the tree and waited. As soon as his feet hit the ground they were on him, holding him down and binding his feet and hands. They dragged him over and roughly dropped him next to her.

Infinity grunted and rolled onto her back. The creatures and their tracking animals stood over them, taking in every detail. One of the bird men let out a long sequence of squawks and chitters.

Suddenly, the tourist opened his mouth and mimicked the series of shrill sounds. The sounds were created by a human mouth, so they certainly weren't exact, but they definitely were similar, and in the same sequence. The bird men went completely still. Infinity turned and stared at Desmond. He had managed to surprise her again.

After several long seconds of silence, the creature the tourist had mimicked took a step closer. It spoke again, a different sequence of bird squawks.

The tourist repeated the sequence, doing a decent job of mimicking every sound except the highest screeches.

11

CURIOSITY

Twelve tracking animals and twelve bird men stared down at Desmond, the latter obviously startled by his attempt to mimic their language. This was good. He had hoped it would make them curious rather than murderous.

The individual that had talked directly to him spoke again, and Desmond again did his best to repeat the sounds. His ability to recall long sequences of information, which was normally of little practical value, was serving him well at this moment. The creatures gathered around closer, and some of them leaned down to gaze at Desmond's face. For the first time, he took note of the finer details of their appearance. Their overall structure was somewhere between a large flightless bird, like an emu, and a theropod dinosaur, like a velociraptor. The bird men stood about five feet tall, although their necks made up at least twelve inches of that height. Their heads were approximately the size of a human head. Round, two-inch eyes capable of gazing straight forward for 3D vision sat near the top of the skull. They had almost no forehead, so their brains, which were obviously well developed, must have been arranged directly behind their faces, near the back of the skull.

Their tan-colored beaks, although smaller than those of the predators Desmond had seen yesterday, were about five inches in both height and length, and had already proven to be formidable. A brown coat of fine feathers covered their entire bodies except for their three-fingered hands and three-toed feet. Their hands, half the size of Desmond's, included two fingers and an opposable thumb, with no visible claws or fingernails. They wore no ornamentation or decorative markings other than lengths of rope and various tools and weapons looped around their necks.

The tracking animals were no more than three feet tall, appearing to be smaller versions of the predators that had attacked Desmond's group minutes after they'd bridged. The trackers' predator-like beaks were proportionally larger than those of their masters. But their overall anatomy was similar: brown coat of feathers, round eyes, three toes, and three fingers, although their toes and fingers ended in black, inch-long claws, obviously better suited to tearing flesh than using tools.

Desmond glanced over at Infinity. She had several new cuts on her arms and legs but otherwise seemed okay. She was staring at him, perhaps trying to decide if he'd gone mad.

Before he could say anything to her, one of the bird men grabbed the ropes on Desmond's ankles and dragged him a few yards. Two others took the ends of ropes that were draped around their necks and tied them to his ankle ropes. They did the same to Infinity's. All of the creatures then turned and walked down the hillside, roughly dragging Desmond and Infinity behind them.

Desmond was able to twist his body several times to avoid being dragged over jagged rocks, but the friction of the bare ground against his skin was already taking a toll. He heard Infinity grunting in pain as she tried to maneuver herself to avoid the worst of the rocks.

When they arrived at the narrow stream at the bottom of the ravine, the creatures dragged Desmond and Infinity into the water and stopped. Several of them stooped over and used their hands to scoop water onto the humans' skin and wipe off the layers of mud. When they revealed the bird tattoo on Infinity's chest, the creatures began another round of staring and talking, as if they were trying to decide exactly what to make of it. The bird men then took turns leaning in to poke and caress the humans' skin, ears, and toes, as well as most of their other parts.

"Be cooperative," Infinity said. "Don't do anything to make them think it's not worth the trouble to keep you alive. Your only goal now is to live until bridge-back. If they plan to kill us, we have to find ways to stall them."

"I think they're curious about us," Desmond said. "They have no idea what we are."

"Then continue to be interesting. Mimicking their speech was good."

Desmond realized the creatures were listening to them talk. Every minute the bird men continued to be curious was one minute closer to bridge-back. "That sounded almost like a compliment," he said, and then he forced himself to laugh out loud. He started with a deep guffaw and ended with a high twitter, sounding completely ridiculous the entire time.

Infinity stared at him. "Are you losing it, tourist?"

"I'm trying to be interesting. They seem fascinated by our voices."

Infinity remained silent for a moment. Suddenly she began chanting, "Hey ho, let's go. Hey ho, let's go. They're forming in a straight line. They're going through a tight wind."

Desmond blinked at her. And then he realized she was singing —or at least trying to "Blitzkrieg Bop" by the Ramones. The bird men watched silently as she continued through the song. Finally she ended with one last, "Hey ho, let's go."

The entire group of creatures continued staring for several seconds. The individual who had spoken to them first—perhaps the leader—emitted a complex series of birdcalls. Several of the others came forward, removed the ropes they'd used to drag the humans down the hill, and tied them around Desmond's and Infinity's necks. Then they removed the restraints from the humans' ankles and handed them to a bird man whose purpose seemed to be carrying heavy coils of rope.

They forced Desmond and Infinity to get to their feet. And then the bird men began making their way up the next hill, pulling the prisoners behind them.

AFTER WHAT MUST HAVE BEEN at least an hour of walking, Desmond began to worry about Infinity. Every step was causing her to grunt, and he could scarcely imagine the pain she was enduring. If she lost consciousness, would the bird men kill her on the spot?

"Wherever we're going, it can't be much farther," he said. "If you need me to, I'll carry you the rest of the way."

She glanced over at him and shook her head but didn't reply.

"They must intend to keep us alive," he said, although he had already decided this was a false hope. If they were being taken somewhere to be butchered and eaten, the bird men would probably rather make them walk than carry their bodies. Also, the longer they were kept alive, the fresher their flesh would be.

Desmond studied the beak of the nearest bird man. It didn't have the look of a predator's beak. It was obviously powerful, but the biting edges lacked serrations. These creatures were either herbivores or omnivores. This was only mildly comforting, considering humans were omnivores and ate plenty of meat.

Desmond noticed they were now walking on a well-worn path, and soon the path was running parallel to a river. It could have been the same river that ran beneath the cave where Lenny and

Xavier were hiding miles away, but if so then here it was wider and deeper. They were still walking through dense forest, but the area across the river opened into a wide, treeless meadow. Several bird men were scattered around the meadow, and Desmond realized it was an agricultural field, planted with waist-high stalks with green bulges at their tips. The bird men were farmers.

One of the bird men leading the humans screeched. This was answered by a similar call from somewhere ahead. Apparently they were approaching their destination. This perhaps meant that rest was within sight for Infinity, but more likely their situation was about to worsen.

Desmond saw an open area ahead, and as they approached it several small creatures in the trees began screeching at them. The bird men ignored this clatter as if they had expected it. Finally, the path opened into a wide, flat riverbank of copper-colored gravel. The river ran along one edge of the gravel, and fifty yards from the water was a vertical cliff face, even taller than the one where they'd left Lenny and Xavier. The cliff extended upstream along the river for at least a quarter mile.

Most striking about the entire scene was that it proved the bird men were far more sophisticated than Desmond had previously guessed. Numerous circular openings to dwellings had been carved into the vertical cliff face, accessible by ladders made of wood and rope, and with rope loops spaced regularly from bottom to top. Dozens of bird people were scattered about on the gravel riverbank working on various tasks. When they noticed the humans, they stopped what they were doing and approached to take a closer look. Several smaller carnivorous pets—the same type as the tracking animals—were milling about. The small, noisy creatures that had fussed at them from the trees came scampering across the gravel, emitting their shrill calls. At the far end of the gravel bar, a massive creature—almost the size of an elephant but on two legs— was dragging a boulder from the cliff face. The creature wore an elaborate rope harness, and two bird men were leading it with leashes.

Bird men surrounded the humans as their captors stopped. Numerous conversations took place at once, sounding like a bird house at a zoo. Desmond and Infinity were prodded and touched all over again, and the creatures pointed at Infinity's bird tattoo as they cackled. Some of the creatures even grabbed them gently with their beaks, tasting their skin with finger-like tongues. This went on for several long minutes.

Two bird men pushed through the onlookers. They each carried a bowl that appeared to have been carved or chewed from solid wood. They both placed the bowls on the ground. One contained water, the other a pile of some kind of seeds or fruit, looking like golf balls covered in green velvet. The bird men used their toes to push the bowls closer to Desmond and Infinity, making it clear they were offering the contents.

"Don't eat the food," Infinity said. "If it's toxic, it could kill you in minutes. But we should drink the water. To keep them happy."

Desmond's arms were tightly bound above the wrists, but he could grasp the bowl and raise it to his mouth. Although speckled with sediment, the water was cool, and he drank it desperately, realizing suddenly how much he needed it. He forced himself to quit when half of it was gone and handed it to Infinity. She finished it off.

One of the bird men nudged the food bowl closer with its toe. Desmond and Infinity ignored it, prompting a round of squawks, whistles, and clicks.

Having apparently come to a consensus, the entire group of bird men and their pets began walking, leaving the bowls behind and pulling Desmond and Infinity with them. They walked upstream along the gravel bar, passing numerous dark openings carved into the cliff, each with a ladder of rope loops and wooden rungs hanging from it. The lower openings were fifteen feet above the gravel bar, probably due to occasional river flooding. Or perhaps as protection from predators.

About halfway between the downstream and upstream ends of the cliff face, Desmond saw a group of five openings that were rectangular instead of circular. Beyond these five were more of the circular openings. The group approached the cluster of rectangular openings and came to a rest directly below them. Everyone grew quiet, as if waiting.

They didn't have to wait long. Dark shapes emerged from three of the rectangular holes almost immediately.

Desmond glanced over at Infinity.

"Remember, be interesting," she said.

The emerging creatures were clearly of a different species. Black feathers, rather than brown, covered their bodies. And they had black beaks, unlike the tan beaks of the brown bird men.

The black birds began descending the ladders, and Desmond realized the rope loops were there to provide a grip for their beaks. Again, he thought of parrots climbing about their cages.

Once they were on the ground, Desmond could see that the black birds were at least as tall as he was, about a foot taller than the brown bird men. But the most remarkable aspect of their appearance was that they were each adorned with dozens of elaborately-beaded cords. They wore them around their necks, chests, arms, and legs. Each cord was strung with objects of alternating colors and shapes: rocks, mollusk shells, insect parts, and other things that were difficult to identify. Against the birds' black feathers, these cords were striking, even beautiful.

The brown bird men and their pets moved aside as the black birds approached and stopped before Desmond and Infinity. Like the others, they had three fingers and three toes. Unlike the brown irises of the smaller birds' eyes, these creatures' irises were black, making it difficult to tell exactly what they were looking at.

One of them spoke. Its squawks and chirps were deeper than

those of the smaller bird people. But apparently the language was the same, because several of the brown birds replied at once. The brown birds went on for minutes, perhaps explaining the circumstances of encountering and catching the humans. As the black birds listened, they stepped forward and began feeling, tasting, and probing.

Finally, one of the black birds interrupted the extensive explanation with a series of cackles and whistles. Seconds later, a brown bird came forward with a weapon. It was a four-foot stick two inches in diameter, with a sharpened stone spearhead attached at each end—a short, double-tipped spear.

This was it, Desmond realized. He and Infinity were about to be killed. He had to recapture their interest. He looked directly at the black bird who had given the order and repeated its last sequence, doing his best to approximate each of the unique sounds.

The three black birds gazed at him. The one he had mimicked gave another order. Several brown birds stepped in and removed all the ropes from the humans' necks and arms. Another brown bird came forward with a second double-tipped spear and handed it to Desmond. The crowd backed up except for the brown bird holding the other weapon, forming a wide circle with Desmond, Infinity, and the armed bird in the center.

"This doesn't look good," Infinity said. "Give me that weapon."

As she spoke, the bird man thrust his spear at Desmond just hard enough to put a small puncture in his thigh.

Desmond slapped his hand over the wound. "That hurt!"

The bird creature held its spear up menacingly.

"They want us to fight," Infinity said. "Give me the damn weapon."

"You're already hurt. You're in no—"

She snatched the spear from him. Without hesitating, she rushed at the armed bird man. At the last moment she crouched down, and with her left hand on the ground she swung her right leg in an arc from the side, knocking the bird's feet from under it. Infinity was already fully erect again by the time the creature thumped onto the ground, and she drove one of the stone tips into its body. In the next three seconds she drove the tip in another five times.

She backed off from the dying creature and turned in a full circle, holding the weapon ready for an almost-certain attack from the other bird men.

12

STUDENTS

Infinity felt like she might pass out. Her drop-sweep had taken the creature down, but it had hurt like hell. Chances were, though, she'd be killed soon and wouldn't have to endure much more. It's obvious the bird men had wanted to watch a fight. Infinity saw only two possible consequences of her quick disposal of their companion: they would become angry and kill her, or they would pit her against another opponent. And another after that. Until she lost. Based on the fact that the bird people were now standing around chattering, the second possibility seemed more likely.

At this point, her goal was to keep the creatures' anger aimed at her rather than at the tourist.

She held her double-tipped weapon ready while the creatures talked, turning frequently in case they tried attacking from behind. Finally, one of the brown birds approached her, unarmed. It extended one hand, all three fingers outstretched, and waited.

She glared at it. "What do you want?"

"He wants you to give him the spear," the tourist said.

The creature curled and straightened its fingers twice, apparently a universal gesture telling her to hand it over.

She sighed and gave the weapon to the bird man, remaining alert in case the creature turned it on her. A second brown bird picked up the weapon next to the creature she'd killed. The two birds brandished the spears at her and Desmond. But instead of attacking, they simply stepped forward and prodded them with the weapons until they started walking.

The crowd parted, allowing Infinity and the tourist to be herded toward the cliff face. The entire pack of creatures followed, forming a semicircle to keep the prisoners from running away. The crowd stopped in front of a fifteen-foot ladder, hanging to the ground from the lowest of the five rectangular cave openings. It was clear the humans were expected to climb the ladder.

"Go on," she said to the tourist. She wasn't going to leave him undefended while she climbed.

The ladder, which had rope loops beside each wooden rung, was made for bird men, not for humans. But the tourist quickly figured it out and climbed to the cave. She followed him up, trying to ignore the grinding agony in her hip.

Once they were at the mouth of the cave, there was nowhere to go but inside. It opened into a single oval chamber about thirty feet deep, with surprisingly smooth walls. The chamber was empty except for a pile of ashes in the center. Apparently these creatures knew how to use fire.

Four of the smaller brown birds had followed them up the ladder, including the two with weapons. The creatures herded them to the back wall of the chamber and then stood squawking to each other.

The tourist sat on the floor and leaned against the rounded wall. "So, what now?"

She groaned and carefully lowered herself beside him. A decent amount of light was coming from the cave's opening, so she inspected the arrow wound on the front of her hip. The mud plug was still in place, but the entire area was swollen. "No idea. But every delay gets us closer to bridge-back."

The four bird men had stopped squawking to watch them talk.

Desmond sighed and leaned his head back against the rock wall. "I guess there's not much chance we can escape."

"Not much."

"I wish we could get back to Lenny and Xavier."

"Not going to happen."

He turned to look at her. "You're a real glass-half-empty person, aren't you?"

"I'm here to keep you alive, not to be an optimist."

"Well, you have accomplished that. So far." He was silent for a few seconds. "They didn't seem too upset when you killed one of their kind. I can't figure these guys out. And what's up with all the biodiversity? If you count the yappy little squirrels and the big draft animal, at least five different species are coexisting here."

"That's your department."

"Aren't you curious about it? You bridge to all these amazing worlds, and you've seen things most people couldn't imagine. Have you really become jaded to it all?"

She gazed at him, and for a moment she imagined how nice it would be if she were with him again at the picnic table on the Safe-Trek grounds. Or in a quiet restaurant. Or any other place where they weren't about to be slaughtered by bird men. She was actually starting to like it when he talked to her, which was worlds away from how she felt about most tourists. Suddenly she realized these were useless thoughts, a waste of the few minutes that might remain of her life. Besides, this tourist's existence to this point had been so different from hers that, beyond their current shared interest in staying alive, they would never have much in common worth talking about.

"It's a job," she said. "Each excursion is a good paycheck, especially if the tourists bridge back in one piece."

"Well, you deserve a bonus for this one."

She decided not to tell him about getting paid double, or about the waiver on penalties for the previous tourist's injuries. Too bad she probably wouldn't live to collect. Her parents would get her salary for five years. Infinity hadn't seen them since she was fourteen, and now she didn't know if they were even alive. If they couldn't be found, the money would go to The Scrapyard, her old training club. The place helped kids who were living on the streets to direct their anger into something productive. It had saved her life —for all that was worth now.

A black bird's head appeared at the ladder. Seconds later it came on up and stood upright in the cave opening. Soon another creature ascended and then stood beside the first. This one, however, was only half the other bird's height. At first Infinity thought it was one of the tracking animals, but it had the same decorative bands, black feathers, and black beak as the larger bird.

"It's a juvenile," the tourist said. "A kid."

Another small one appeared, and then another. They kept coming until about twenty were standing in a semicircle around the two humans. Only a third of them were black. The rest were brown with tan beaks.

The adult black bird began squawking and clicking. It continued for several minutes. When it stopped, the kids stepped closer to Infinity and Desmond. The brown adults with spears raised their weapons, threatening to use them if the humans tried anything. The kids leaned in and touched the humans' skin, rubbing their tiny fingers over them and chittering to each other.

And then the kids were ordered back to the ladder, and they all climbed down, followed by the black adult. The lesson—or whatever it had been—was over.

"This just keeps getting weirder," the tourist said.

"Every minute helps."

A screech came from the ground below. Abruptly, the four

brown guards forced Infinity and Desmond to their feet and over to the ladder. They all descended to the gravel bar, and the guards led them to the spot where Infinity had killed the bird man. The creature's body was gone, and a heavy boulder had been dragged to the spot where it had died. A thick-legged, elephant-sized beast like the one they'd seen earlier stood nearby, adorned with a rope harness, which explained how the massive rock had been moved.

The bird people quickly gathered around again, as if something important were about to happen. This time the young brown and black birds were part of the crowd. Infinity had a sickening feeling the kids had been brought here to witness something unpleasant.

A pair of brown birds emerged from the crowd, each of them wielding one of the two-tipped weapons, apparently ready to fight.

"Here we go again," the tourist said.

"You stay to the side. I'll handle this." She watched the armed creatures, trying to come up with a strategy to surprise them both.

The armed bird men didn't advance. Instead, they waited while a black bird came forward, went to the boulder, and pushed aside some of the gravel beneath it. This exposed the stone tip of another spear. The bird men had buried it beneath several inches of gravel and then dragged the boulder over it, pinning it beneath the ground. Another black bird appeared, dragging a short, thick log with one hand and carrying a long wooden pole in the other. It dropped both of these items, and then both black birds backed away.

The armed brown birds immediately lunged at Infinity, thrusting their weapons but pulling them back before touching her.

"It's a test." The tourist said. "They're trying to figure out how smart we are."

One of the brown birds circled to Infinity's side, brandishing its spear.

"No shit," she said. She considered simply grabbing the long pole and taking out the two armed birds with it, forgoing the damn puzzle. But she had a gut feeling that wouldn't help the tourist survive until bridge-back. "I'll keep these two busy," she said. "You get me that weapon." From the corner of her eye, she saw the tourist kick the log closer to the boulder and then grab the wooden pole. The two brown birds still hadn't attacked, and Infinity wondered if they were there only to force her and the tourist to solve the idiotic puzzle.

"I need help!" The tourist had wedged the end of the pole under the boulder and over the log. He was now practically hanging from the other end of the pole, but this was barely moving the boulder.

Keeping her eye on the two birds, she went to the pole and helped pull it down, prying the edge of the boulder off the ground. It took both of them to hold the boulder up, so neither of them could release the pole to retrieve the weapon.

"Let it down," Desmond said. "We pushed it back a little. We'll just keep doing it until it's off the spear."

The two birds could easily have attacked at this moment, but they remained in place—more evidence that their purpose was simply to provide incentive.

The humans pried the boulder up again, moving it a few more inches. The armed birds moved in closer and hovered behind them menacingly. Infinity and the tourist pried the boulder a third time, and then a fourth. The spear was now exposed, so they lowered the rock and Infinity rushed to the weapon and pulled it from the gravel.

She stepped away from the boulder and raised the spear over her head. "Is this what you wanted to see, dumbasses?"

The two armed birds charged. She swiped at one of their spears, knocking it off course, but the other caught her shoulder, tearing open the flesh. Why were they attacking now? This whole scenario made no sense. "Call them off!" she cried. "We figured out your stupid puzzle."

"Look out!" Desmond shouted.

The two birds were coming at her again, but this time one was behind the other. She blocked the leading bird's weapon and buried the tip of her own in the creature's side. The bird went down immediately and began writhing. Her weapon was firmly embedded, so she grabbed the fallen bird's spear to face the second attacker.

An ear-splitting screech stopped the oncoming bird. A black bird emerged from the crowd, pulled the weapon from the injured brown bird, rolled the bird over with one foot, and then ran the weapon through its back. It immediately stopped moving. The other brown bird lowered its weapon and backed away.

The black bird took a few steps toward Infinity. She readied her weapon, preparing for a more serious attack. But the black bird stopped, extended a hand, and curled its fingers twice.

Infinity didn't offer her weapon. "I've had enough of this game. Why don't you take it from me?"

"Infinity, every minute counts. Don't fight until you have to."

She glanced at him. The damn tourist was right. Slowly, she stood up straight and handed over the weapon.

SEVERAL MINUTES later they were back in the chamber carved into the cliff face. A group of brown birds appeared and offered another bowl of water, and the humans both drank. The creatures also offered a bowl of food, this time containing what looked like raw meat. Again, Infinity told the tourist to refuse it.

The tourist stared at the bowl of glistening flesh. "Why do I get the impression this meat is from one of the two bird men you've killed since we arrived?"

"I killed one. They killed the other one themselves." This fact was disturbing to Infinity. Not because it was necessarily bad news, but because it had been unexpected. She hated unpredictable adversaries. Most humans—except for the truly psychotic—were predictable and therefore could be defeated. But these bird creatures didn't think anything like humans.

The tourist said, "The larger black birds don't seem to care about the lives of the brown ones. Maybe the brown ones are slaves and are considered disposable."

"Slaves aren't disposable. I'd think they'd usually be in short supply, and they require feeding and training."

"Valid point. Also, most of the young ones they brought to observe us were brown. It doesn't seem likely that slave children would be educated alongside the children of the masters."

Infinity glanced up at the four brown birds assigned as guards. "Listen, tourist. Before, I said we needed to keep them interested in us. Well, they are, and maybe that's why we're still alive. But I doubt they're finished testing us. If whatever comes next involves fighting or killing more of them, that's my job. I don't know what they want from us, but I do know that if they're going to hate one of us for killing their fighters, it should be me."

He sighed. "I know, to maximize my chances of living to bridgeback. I get it. But also consider that they might gain respect for you with every bird man you kill. And if I just sit on the sidelines, where does that leave me?" He looked at her in a way that almost made her break her gaze. "But here's the deal," he said. "We've been through a lot together, and I'm getting kind of attached to you. Maybe you're a bridger, but you're also a human being. It's bad enough that Razor is dead. I don't care to live the rest of my life knowing you also died trying to save my sorry ass. Why should your life be worth less than mine?"

She looked away for a moment and then turned back to face him. "You need to let me do my job, tourist," she said firmly.

"I'd rather you call me Desmond. You bridgers use *tourist* like it's derogatory."

A screech came from outside the chamber. The four guards prodded them to get up and move to the opening.

"Okay, Desmond," she said. "Let me do my job, and maybe we'll *both* live to bridge-back."

INFINITY HAD BEEN RIGHT, the birds intended to test them again. And the young birds—the students—were front and center in the audience. High above, a rope had been suspended from the top of the cliff. Two of the short, double-tipped spears had been tied to the end of the rope about twenty feet above the gravel bar. The crowd formed a circle around the humans, and several black birds came forward and dropped some materials on the ground: three poles, each about ten feet long, a coiled length of thin rope, a pile of short sticks, and a jagged-edged rock.

"It's another ridiculously-simple puzzle," Desmond said. "Maybe they think we got lucky before. They can't quite believe we're actually intelligent."

Infinity gazed up at the hanging spears. "Or maybe this is the most complicated puzzle their little bird brains can come up with."

The crowd became quiet, watching and waiting. Infinity gazed around at them until she saw what she was expecting—the spear-wielding birds who would force them to solve the puzzle. But this time there were three of them. They came forward, ready to attack.

So far these creatures hadn't shown any great level of skill with their weapons, and there was a decent chance she could disarm one of them and kill all three. But what good would that do? The birds could be replaced by more, and still she and the tourist would be forced to solve the damn puzzle.

She glanced at the tourist while also trying to keep an eye on the armed bird men. Desmond had already picked up the coiled rope and was staring at the other materials.

Desmond said, "We can't make a ladder with what we have here, but we can tie the three poles end-to-end to make one long pole. Then we can lean it against the cliff, and I can shinny up it and untie the spears."

Infinity grabbed one of the ten-foot poles and placed it next to another with two feet of overlap. "This is a chance to gain time. Don't rush it."

He nodded. "Got it." He then began slowly wrapping the rope around the overlapping poles.

After about ten loops, they worked together to pull the rope tight and knot it. Then they overlapped the third pole with the second. The coil of rope was one long strand, so they had to trail it about seven feet from the first knot to the juncture of the second and third poles. But this didn't leave enough rope to wrap the poles adequately.

Infinity got off her knees and stood straight up to relieve the pain in her hip. She glared at the three armed birds. She was getting sick of being forced to perform tricks. The birds, sensing she was becoming defiant, stepped forward and held the stone tips of their weapons in her face.

"Take this," the tourist said. He held out the jagged rock the birds had provided. She took it from him, and he grabbed the rope and held it against the gravel. "Cut right there."

Aware that three spears were inches from the back of her head, she struck the rope repeatedly with the rock's edge until it was severed. The tourist took the loose end, moved to the third pole, and began wrapping.

But then he paused. "This may not work." He unwrapped the third pole, got up, and hoisted the first two attached poles until they were vertical. He leaned the entire thing against the rock face. It was still six feet shy of the two hanging weapons, but he spit on his hands, rubbed them together, and started climbing. Infinity stepped up and held the pole steady, to prevent it from falling to the left or right. When he had ascended past the joint between the two poles, the top pole started slipping through the knotted loops. The rope wasn't tight enough. He dropped to the ground and stared at the poles. "Well, that didn't work. This is going to take longer than I thought. Fortunately for us, I guess."

A wave of chatter worked its way around the onlooking crowd. Suddenly, the exit wound on Infinity's hip exploded with fiery pain, so intense that she cried out and fell to her knees. She knew she was in danger, but for several seconds she couldn't even focus her eyes.

"Get away from her!" The tourist was standing over her but throbbing static in her ears made his voice sound distant.

She shook her head and bit her lip, trying to get through the worst of it.

"Infinity, are you okay?"

As the seconds passed, the pain began to recede. She reached back and touched the arrow's exit wound. Her hand came away red with blood. One of the birds had snuck up on her and shoved its spear directly into the wound. At the very least, the mud plug had been dislodged. She looked up at the armed birds. They stood there, weapons ready. Blood covered the spear tip of the one nearest her. Even if she did nothing else, she would kill that bastard.

"Infinity?"

"I'm still here," she said. "I don't think we're solving the puzzle fast enough for them. I'm going to stay down—make them believe I'm too hurt to get up. Get me those goddamn spears! Retie the ropes around the poles loosely, and then use a stick to cinch it so tight it won't slip."

"I'm on it." He rushed to the poles and got to work.

Infinity's pain was subsiding, but it was replaced by waves of nausea. She groaned and focused on getting it under control.

The bird with the bloody spearhead began moving toward her

again. She tracked its movements from the corner of her eye without raising her head. When the creature was only a few feet away, it let out several soft murmurs, sounding almost like a lamb. It slowly raised its spear tip and moved it toward Infinity's throbbing wound, like it was taunting her—threatening her with more pain.

As she watched the roughly-carved stone spearhead inch its way closer, she briefly considered the consequences of giving in to her anger. The tourist—Desmond—had to survive until bridge-back. It was becoming increasingly likely that she wouldn't make it, but he had to. She'd never lost a tourist before, and she wasn't going to now. Not this tourist.

The spear tip was inches from her wound, and she saw the bird's arm muscles tense up to thrust it in.

She swung her arm, knocking the weapon's tip upward, and dove for the bird's feet. She then tucked herself into a somersault, her legs knocking the bird onto its back. She continued her roll until she was sitting on the creature's abdomen. It flailed its hands, still holding the spear, but the weapon was too long for close-quarters fighting. Infinity ignored the spear and pinned the bird's neck to the gravel with her left hand. She immediately started throwing jabs at the bird's head with her right fist, aiming for the closest of its two eyes and twisting her chest to put as much power into each blow as she could.

She had always had a habit of silently counting off the blows whenever she used this attack. This time she reached sixteen before realizing the bird was no longer struggling. She grabbed the bird's weapon and leapt to her feet, grunting from the pain.

The other two armed birds hadn't attacked. Without any attempt to interfere, they had watched their companion get beaten to a pulp. Infinity was alive because of their indifference, but she didn't understand it. Their behavior made no sense.

Desmond stood up. He had finished tying the poles together and cinching the ropes tight. He seemed to notice for the first time that Infinity was now holding a weapon. "Um, I was going to say this is ready, but I guess we don't need the spears now?"

"I have no idea what we're supposed to do."

The two remaining armed birds moved toward Desmond.

Infinity stepped into their path, cutting them off. The birds stopped advancing and stood there holding their spears out menacingly. "Apparently they're not going to quit until we get those weapons." Keeping an eye on the two birds, she used her free hand to help him lift the three-section pole and lean it against the rock. The end of it was now several feet higher than the dangling spears.

Desmond tried swinging the pole back and forth to knock the spears loose, but the pole was heavy and unwieldy, and the spears were apparently tied securely.

"You're going to have to climb," Infinity said. She held the pole steady with her free hand, still watching the armed birds.

He shinnied up the pole surprisingly fast for a man with no clothing over his groin. When he got to the top, he wrapped his legs around the pole to hold himself in place and untied the spears, letting them fall. Infinity snatched them up, and he slid down most of the way and then dropped to the ground beside her.

Another flurry of conversation ran through the onlooking birds. A black bird came forward and held a hand out to Infinity for her to give up the weapons.

She shook her head and handed them over. "What, you're not going to make us kill another of your buddies?"

The moment the bird took the spears, three unarmed brown birds rushed Infinity. Before she could react, they had grabbed her arms and ankles with their hands and beaks, knocking her to the ground. She tried to struggle, but the birds' beaks were clamped down so hard they threatened to snap her bones. She looked over at Desmond. He had been forced back against the rock wall by the two armed brown birds.

"Don't do anything aggressive unless they actually try to kill you!" she shouted. "When that happens, scream at them like a maniac and then break through the crowd and run. Run like hell!"

He stared at the spear tips held inches from his chest. "I don't know if I can."

"You can and you will!"

The black bird walked to Desmond, handed him one of the spears, and moved back into the crowd of onlookers.

Desmond's eyes were wide. "What am I supposed to do with this?"

Infinity realized what was happening. "Let me up!" She kicked and spat and growled at the birds holding her down, but they only tightened their grip. "Desmond, they're making you fight!"

"I have no idea how to fight."

"You've got no choice! Listen to my voice but don't look at me. I'll tell you what to do and when to do it."

The two armed birds crouched and held their weapons ready.

13

PLANS

Until recently, Desmond hadn't had many encounters with violence in his life. Before this excursion, he had only hit one person with real intent to do harm. That had been in 6th grade, and it hadn't ended well for Desmond. He was currently in good physical shape, but he had never taken martial arts or boxing lessons, and he hadn't served in the military. Now he was being forced to fight for his life.

Instinctively he stepped back from the two armed bird men, but his back hit solid rock.

"Tell me you hear my voice, tourist!"

"I hear you. But I don't see how—"

"Listen! You have two things going for you. These bastards don't know what we're saying, and they don't understand how we think. You have to surprise them."

The two birds were close, but they were waiting for him to make the first move. What would happen if he simply refused to fight? He straightened up and lowered his weapon.

The birds thrust their spears simultaneously, puncturing his left shoulder and his chest.

"Goddammit!" he cried, raising his spear again. He felt warm blood flowing over his skin, but he didn't dare look down at his wounds.

"They could have killed you just then, but they didn't," Infinity said. "They want to see what you can do."

"I can't do anything!"

"The bird man on your right was careless. He came at you with his weapon in front of him instead of to the side. Listen up. Get him to thrust again. Then do this in one motion: release your weapon, grab his with both hands, and run at him with everything you've got. Keep his weapon tip to your side, not in front of you. And scream when you do it."

Desmond realized his hands were shaking. "Oh, God. I'll try." He lowered his spear again.

The birds responded the same way they had the first time—they jabbed and punctured his skin. This time, he dropped his spear, grabbed the weapon that had just gouged his chest, and rushed forward, screaming uncontrollably.

He shoved the bird back several steps until it fell onto its back. Desmond raised his end of the spear and drove the other end into the creature, actually lifting his own feet off the ground as he put all his weight on the shaft.

"Don't stop moving! Throw the weapon at the other bird, grab your own weapon, and swing it instead of thrusting. *Kill* the son of a bitch!"

Desmond's adrenaline had taken over. It seemed his body was beyond his control, blindly following Infinity's commands. He yanked the spear from the fallen bird and heaved it at the one that was still standing. Without waiting to see the result of his throw, he rushed back and snapped up his dropped spear. He ran at the standing bird, swinging the spear wildly. The bird had just finished deflecting the thrown spear and was recovering its balance when the side of Desmond's weapon struck it's neck. The creature lost its balance again, and Desmond swung the spear straight down on the top of its head with a solid hit.

The next few seconds were a frantic blur. Desmond swung the weapon over and over, pummeling the creature. He heard himself grunting and cursing, but it felt like someone else was using his voice to make these sounds.

Suddenly he was on his back. Tiny hands and crushing beaks held him in place. He struggled furiously to escape.

"Desmond! Stop fighting!"

Infinity's voice pierced his feral rage. He relaxed his arms and legs. He blinked at the shapes holding him down. Brown bird men, at least four of them. And two of the larger black birds were standing over them.

"Okay, okay," he said. "You can let go."

Of course they couldn't understand him. But one at a time they released him and stepped back. He sat up.

"I'm impressed, tourist." Infinity had been released and was also sitting up.

He looked over at the second bird he'd attacked. It was dead, beyond any doubt. The first bird was still sprawled on the gravel. It was holding its wound with both hands and staring at Desmond.

One of the black birds picked up the spear Desmond had used as a deadly club. It walked over to the injured brown bird, kicked it until it rolled onto its belly, and then drove the spear through its back.

"THIS ISN'T GOING to end until we're dead, is it?" Desmond said. Once again they were back in the chamber carved out of the cliff face, with the same four guards watching them. Desmond was still trembling from the recent fight. His entire body was covered in scratches and bruises. His nose was still tender to the touch from having slammed into his knee the previous day. And now he had four new puncture wounds to add to his collection. Fortunately they weren't terribly deep, and the bleeding had nearly stopped.

"Or until bridge-back," Infinity said. She was pressing her hand on her newly-opened hip wound. Blood was trickling through her fingers.

"Lean over. Let me look at that."

She leaned onto her side, and Desmond shifted his body so he wasn't blocking the light from the cave opening. The blood flowing from the wound was speckled with bits of mud. Apparently the bird's spear tip had shredded the leaf casing that was supposed to keep the mud contained, mashing the mud into the wound. It looked horrific.

"I think the bleeding is slowing down," he said. "You'll be okay."

She rolled back to a sitting position and nodded like she was trying to convince herself he wasn't lying. "My sense of time is starting to blur, but I think we're well into the afternoon. If we're lucky, bridge-back will be in three or four hours."

Desmond stared at his fingers and tried to stop trembling. "Why did you tell me to swing the spear instead of stabbing?"

She glanced at him, frowning. "Because they wouldn't expect it. It worked, didn't it?"

He huffed out a nervous laugh and nodded. "I can't believe I lived through that fight."

"They weren't trying to kill you."

"Then what are they trying to do? This whole sick game is costing them lives."

"It's only costing the lives of the brown birds."

He looked at her, considering this. "You think this is all for the black birds' amusement?"

"Maybe. Or maybe for some other purpose, but the black birds are definitely running the show."

A now-familiar screech came from the gravel bar below. As expected, the four guards prodded them to their feet.

THE CROWD WAS STILL GATHERED, including the children. Six black adults stood chattering to each other apart from the brown birds, but they joined the crowd when Desmond and Infinity arrived at the site of the recent fights. Desmond saw blood stains on the gravel, but the bodies of the dead brown birds had been removed.

A black bird approached and placed four items on the ground at the humans' feet: a coiled length of rope, one of the short, double-tipped spears, a knife with a stone blade, and one of the weird crossbow-like weapons that had injured Infinity.

Desmond gazed at the objects. "Well, at least we don't have to retrieve a spear this time."

"Don't celebrate just yet, tourist. They might make us fight each other. I had a feeling this was coming."

His chest tightened, and he felt a wave of nausea. "I'm not going to do that."

"No, you're not."

He frowned at her. What did she mean by that?

Before he could ask, the crowd abruptly parted. Two black birds stood there gazing at Desmond and Infinity, each with a double-tipped spear in one hand and three other items looped around its neck: a rope, a knife, and a crossbow. The same set of items given to the humans. And in front of each black bird a smaller tracking animal strained at its leash, shaking with excitement.

One of the black birds cackled and whistled. The crowd formed another opening on the side opposite the two armed black birds. The two bird men and their pets began moving toward the humans.

Suddenly the pieces fell together in Desmond's mind. This was why the brown birds hadn't killed them. It was why the black birds were so interested in what he and Infinity were capable of. The black birds wanted to pursue them—to hunt them. For entertainment, perhaps. Or for training. Or it could have even been some kind of twisted religious ritual.

Infinity gathered up the four items and handed Desmond the rope and crossbow. "This is a good thing."

"In what way is this good?" he said as they began backing away from the approaching creatures.

"Now you don't have to kill me."

He shot a glance at her.

"And," she continued, "they don't know we're disappearing in several hours. If they really let us run, we have a chance."

It certainly looked like the bird people were letting them leave the village. The creatures made no attempt to interfere as they backed through the gap in the crowd. The downstream end of the vertical cliff was several hundred yards beyond the crowd, and no bird men blocked their way.

The two black birds and their pets began walking faster. They were no more than thirty yards from the humans.

Desmond looked at Infinity. Her rigid expression showed that walking was painful. "Can you run?" he asked.

"I can outrun *you*. But they expect us to run. So we're swimming instead. You can swim, right?"

"What? Yes, I can—"

"Follow me and stay close."

She took off abruptly, veering away from the cliff. Desmond followed. By the time they reached the river's edge, the crowd had begun screeching and whistling. Desmond looped the coiled rope over his shoulder as they waded into the river. He forced himself to ignore the agony of walking on the large rocks of the river bed. When the water was waist deep, he followed Infinity's lead and leaned forward to let the current carry him.

When they were about halfway across, perhaps twenty yards out, Desmond turned to look back. The black birds and their pets were standing at the riverbank watching them. The current was slow enough that the birds could have kept up by walking the shore, but they stayed where they were. It was probably useless to try guessing their intentions, but he was pretty sure they weren't going to let their captives get away this easily. Still, perhaps if he and Infinity let the river carry them a mile or two, the tracking animals would fail to find where they exited the water.

"Dammit!" Infinity's head jerked around, her arms thrashing.

Desmond noticed prickly pain on his chest and arm, and suddenly he understood. "Get out!" he cried.

Infinity was already swimming furiously for the shore opposite the bird men, but she was still holding the spear and knife, which slowed her down. Desmond was behind her and trying to keep up. The rope hanging from his shoulder and the crossbow in one hand made swimming impossible, so he resorted to walking in the chest-deep water. Every few seconds he swiped his free hand at carnivorous fish feeding on his wounds. Soon the fish were biting other parts of his body, including his groin. He gave up trying to swipe them away, and he put every ounce of effort into reaching the shore.

By the time he crawled onto the rocks, Infinity was already sitting up inspecting red bite marks, which dotted most of her body. Desmond was no better off. He had countless tiny bites, a thin trickle of blood running from each one. Two of the fish were still clamped onto the raw tissue where the bird's weapons had punctured his chest. He angrily crushed them between his fingers as he pulled them off.

"I'd kill for a pair of shoes and some clothes," he said. He looked across the river. The black birds were still at the water's edge, perhaps forty yards away. They chattered to each other while gazing across at the humans. They seemed calm, as if they found the situation only mildly interesting.

Infinity moaned as she got to her feet. "They want us to run, to get a head start. But my body's almost done. There's no way we can lose those tracking creatures. So I have a plan, and I don't want any crap from you. We'll cross this field and I'll find a place where I can ambush them. I've got one fight left in me. I may be able to take them both out. Regardless, I want you to be two miles away by the time they find me. With that kind of lead, you might last until bridge-back." She nodded toward the forest on the far side of the birds' crop field. "When we get to those trees, you're going to take off, and I'm going to hide and wait for the bastards. Let's go." She turned and started walking across the birds' crop field.

Desmond got to his feet and stood there for a moment, considering Infinity's plan. He shook his head and caught up to her. But he remained silent. He definitely wasn't going to leave her alone, so there was no point in arguing about it.

ALL DESMOND COULD SEE of Infinity was her eyes, and she was still glaring at him. She was twenty yards away, against the ground and well hidden in some low brush. Desmond was hidden in the same way. It was all part of Infinity's plan, except that Desmond wasn't two miles away running for his life.

Once Infinity had given up on convincing Desmond to leave her, she had picked a spot with brush on both sides. They had walked through the middle of it and continued on for about fifty yards before splitting up and circling back on either side. When the tracking animals led the black birds on the scent trail between the two hiding spots, Infinity and Desmond would let them pass and then surprise them by attacking from behind. Infinity had given him the spear, keeping the knife for herself.

After having defeated the two brown birds back at the cliff, Desmond was feeling confident. He planned to swing the spear as a club, as he had done before, and after the first hit he would thrust one of the stone tips into the bird until it was dead. He had no idea if the tracking animals were dangerous, but they would probably have to kill those, too.

Now all they had to do was wait. If the black birds didn't show up—even better.

No such luck. Desmond heard them chattering to each other before they came into view. The damn things were awfully casual about this hunt, probably due to overconfidence. Desmond was looking forward to shutting them up for good.

Just as Infinity had predicted, a few minutes later the birds passed directly between them, the tracking animals bent low against their leashes, following the scent trail. Desmond's heart began beating faster, and his hands started shaking, his self-assurance having quickly evaporated. He'd had one lucky win against creatures that weren't even trying to kill him. How could he have thought he was now a real fighter?

The creatures walked past, and Desmond saw movement in the brush on the opposite side of the path. Infinity was nodding at him. It was time.

She struggled to her feet and charged the black bird nearest her.

Feeling again as if his mind were disconnected from his own body, Desmond charged the other bird man at full speed. Infinity had said to be silent until he had made the first cut, but he involuntarily screamed in raw fury.

He swung his weapon at the bird's head but it swished through the air without making contact, and he lost his balance. The bird had ducked just in time. Before Desmond knew what was happening, he was on his back. The black bird was standing over him, pressing one of the points of its spear into his throat. The bird's tracking animal was inches from Desmond's face, sniffing his scent but remaining eerily silent.

"Don't try to fight!" Infinity cried. "Don't even move—we underestimated these assholes."

Desmond turned his head to see her. She was on her back also, the other black bird pinning her to the ground in the same way.

The two birds squawked back and forth briefly. Hoping it might help, Desmond did his best to repeat the same squawks.

The bird above him leaned closer, its unblinking black eyes studying him. It pulled the spear tip back from his throat and slowly moved it down to the middle of his chest and then to the side, the point barely touching Desmond's skin as it moved. The tip stopped, hovering just above one of the puncture wounds he'd received earlier. The tip entered the wound, gradually pushing its way into his already tender flesh.

He tried not to struggle. "No, please don't."

The bird savagely raked the spear tip up toward Desmond's shoulder, ripping through skin and muscle on the right side of his chest.

He screamed and slammed his head on the ground. He grabbed the spear, which was already pressing against his throat again.

Just then, Infinity screamed also, her cry ending with garbled curses Desmond couldn't understand.

He turned and saw that the black bird standing over her had run its spear entirely through the arrow wound in her hip, grinding the spear's tip into the soil beneath her. Without warning, it yanked the spear back out, and she screamed again.

With incapacitating horror, Desmond realized the birds were not only going to kill them—they were going to make them suffer. The creatures seemed fascinated with their reactions to being tormented. Perhaps it was their way of studying creatures they didn't understand.

Desmond grabbed the bird's spear and pulled it closer to his own throat. "Just kill me!"

"No, Desmond!" Infinity said. "Don't you dare."

The bird yanked the spear from his hands. It stepped back, pulling its tracking animal with it. It then pointed its spear to the forest, in the direction Desmond and Infinity had been fleeing before their failed ambush.

Desmond grunted and got to his feet. Infinity rolled over to her hands and knees but was struggling to stand up. He went over and helped her.

"They're letting us go," he said. "Again."

She nodded. "Then let's go."

One of the black birds squawked. Desmond turned, and the creature pointed its spear toward the stone knife Infinity had dropped and then to Desmond's spear. Desmond picked them up. The bird then gripped the crossbow and coil of rope hanging from its neck and shook them. Desmond sighed, walked to his hiding spot, and retrieved his crossbow and rope. The two birds watched calmly as he turned back to Infinity.

He put her arm over his shoulder and together they walked through the forest until they could no longer see the black birds.

"Change of plans," Infinity said. Her uneven words indicated that every step was a battle. "We can't fight them. They'll beat us again. And if we live, again after that."

"That's not much of a plan."

She shot him a glance, sweat running down her face. "It's simple. You endure whatever they do to you."

14

CREED

Heart to blood, muscle to bone, tourist flesh above my own.
With self-sacrifice near, my fuel is fear.
By bridger means and might, tourists will not fight.
There were two more lines, but Infinity couldn't remember them. She had repeated the five principles of the Bridger's Creed hundreds of times—maybe thousands—but at this moment she couldn't remember the last two.

"Are you okay?" the tourist asked. "You're mumbling." He had his arm around her waist, helping her walk.

She nodded. "I'm fine." But why couldn't she remember the last two principles? In fact, she felt as if the first three were about to slip away too. *Heart to blood, muscle to bone, tourist flesh above my own. With self-sacrifice near, my fuel is fear. By bridger means and might... By bridger means and might...*

"We need to get you some water," said the tourist—the tourist who should never have had to fight.

That was it. *By bridger means and might, tourists will not fight.*

"Just hang on. The river's this way. We'll get you hydrated. You've lost a lot of blood."

He was walking faster than she could move her feet and she stumbled. "This isn't right," she said. "I'm a liability."

He continued pulling her along. "It's a bridging excursion. You take what you get."

"That's stupid."

"You're the one who said it, Infinity. Two days ago."

Heart to blood, muscle to bone, tourist flesh above my own.

"I see the water now. You'll drink, we'll cross the river again, and then we'll lose them."

She stumbled again. "I've got a better plan."

"Just save it. Your plans always involve getting yourself killed. I'm not letting that happen."

The river was bordered here by tall mud banks, so they walked downstream until they found a washout they could easily descend. With his arm still around her waist, the tourist walked her into the current until they were thigh deep.

"Drink as much as you can."

She put her entire head under for several seconds, allowing the cool water to rinse away the sweat and filth. Then she drank until she felt like she might throw up. Several carnivorous fish had already found her and were nibbling at her flesh, but at this point they were a minor annoyance.

The tourist looked back the way they'd come. "No sign of them yet. Let's drift downstream a ways and then cross."

Her head was clearer now. "That's what *you're* going to do, but I'm going ashore here. I'll walk upstream, and they'll follow my scent trail. Get as far as you can."

He frowned, then grimaced and swiped at a fish biting his leg. "Listen, bridger. Five minutes ago you could barely walk. You won't get far. They'll find you in no time. Then they'll realize what our plan was and come after me. I heard some of what you were mumbling. *By bridger means and might, tourists will not fight.* If you leave me alone, you'll be forcing me to fight alone. So you need to do your goddamn job and come with me."

She glared at him. He was right—she wouldn't get far. But he wouldn't get far either, dragging her with him. She looked down at the stone knife she was still gripping in her right hand. There was one way she could make him flee without her. *With self-sacrifice near, my fuel is fear.* She raised the knife to her throat.

"Don't!" he gasped. "You're the only thing keeping me going."

She blinked. Slowly, she lowered the knife. Carnivorous fish were still picking at her wounds, but she didn't care. As a bridger she had made difficult decisions before, but she had never felt this uncertain. Her gut instinct told her that self-sacrifice was the right thing for this situation, but Desmond was also right. Or did she just *want* him to be right?

"Okay," she whispered.

He furrowed his brows, and his shoulders relaxed slightly.

"I said *okay.* Let's move."

They waded farther into the water and allowed the current to carry them downstream, but soon the biting fish became intolerable, forcing them to cross the river.

Infinity kept a good pace for a few minutes, but then she began stumbling again, and Desmond had to support her. Every step with her right leg sent spasms through her hip. She realized that if Desmond weren't with her she would have already given up and stopped to make one last stand against the black bird men.

Step after burning step she pushed on. They followed the river so that Infinity could replenish her depleted fluids as needed. They hadn't seen the bird men since before crossing the river, but Infinity knew it was only a matter of time. And the sun was still too high to allow for hope that bridge-back would occur first.

Desmond stopped abruptly, snapping Infinity out of a pain-ridden stupor.

"Stay still," he whispered.

She followed his gaze. About sixty yards to their left, three beaked, wolf-sized animals were hungrily feeding on a large carcass. The mangled corpse was impaled beneath a wooden framework of spikes.

"I've been here before," he said softly. "That's the kill trap I told you about yesterday. I know where we are."

The creatures continued tearing at the carcass, apparently unaware of the humans. Desmond guided Infinity down the sloping bank of the river until they were out of the creatures' sight. They moved downstream a short distance and then started back up the bank toward the trees.

Infinity tripped and fell, bringing Desmond down with her. It felt good to lie still on the muddy slope. "I'm done, tourist. You gotta leave me here."

Desmond put a hand on her shoulder. "Listen. Like I said, I know where we are. We're going over this hill and up the next. That's where the cave is." He patted the length of rope coiled around his shoulder. "We're going to drop down to the cave and hide there until bridge-back."

"They'll track us there, straight to your friends," she said.

"But the cave is defensible, right?"

She considered this. The black bird men would have to lower themselves to the cave by rope. Even if they could do that with one hand and a beak, they would be vulnerable. If she could make it to the cave, she could lower Desmond and the weapons down, and all three tourists would have a reasonable chance. Particularly if she then lured the bird men away from the cave.

She nodded. "Okay."

He got to his feet and then helped her up. They began making their way toward the cave.

But by the time they reached the first hill's summit, Infinity knew she wasn't going to make it. No amount of willpower could overcome her exhaustion and the paralyzing pain that came with every step.

She could tell that the tourist knew it, too. Every few seconds he would look over his shoulder to see if the bird men were catching up, and as they began descending the slope to the next valley, he stopped.

"Take these." He handed her the two-tipped spear he'd been carrying in his free hand. He had also been carrying the knife since she'd dropped it near the river, and he handed it to her as well. "Yesterday, you carried Lenny over your shoulders. That's what I'm going to do now."

She studied him for a moment. Was he strong enough to pull it off? Would it get him into the cave faster? She wasn't sure, but she couldn't think clearly enough to argue.

"Okay." She transferred the two weapons to her left hand and swung the crossbow around so it was hanging against her back. "Take my right hand in your left and put my arm over your shoulders."

He had to bend over to do this.

"Now put your right arm between my legs and pick me up."

He bent lower, grunted, and used his legs to lift her. Without needing to be told, he transferred her right wrist to his right hand and gripped it tightly. "Jesus, you're heavier than you look."

"Shut up and walk. Look before you place every step. With a heavy load, your balance will suck."

He started down the hill, stumbling a few times at first but quickly finding a rhythm.

Heart to blood, muscle to bone, tourist flesh above my own. With self-sacrifice near, my fuel is fear. By bridger means and might, tourists will not fight. Infinity still couldn't recall the last two. But it didn't really matter—at this moment she was probably defying all of them.

Exhausted, she allowed her head to hang down and rest against

Desmond's arm. Briefly, she wondered if her name would be added to the Lost Bridger wall in the hallway of SafeTrek if she didn't make it. Maybe they'd put hers beneath Hornet's and Razor's.

Desmond slogged through the stream at the bottom of the first hill and started up the second hill. The rhythm of his steps and his breathing lulled Infinity toward unconsciousness.

"We made it," the tourist said after what seemed like a long time.

Infinity opened her eyes and blinked. He was right—they were at the top of the hill.

He kneeled and gently rolled her onto the ground. Again he put a reassuring hand on her shoulder. "You still with me?"

She nodded and sat up. The knife and spear were still in her left hand. Sprawled on the ground beside her like a dead snake was the rope they had made the previous day.

She nodded at the longer rope still hanging from his shoulder. "Give me that. We're getting you down to the cave."

He lifted the rope from his shoulder. "We'll figure out a way to fasten it to something, and we'll *both* go."

She looked around. There was nothing there but a few loose rocks, none of them large enough to support either of them. She looked at the four-foot spear. Could they drive it into the ground and tie off to it? Was it strong enough? She handed it to him. "This is all we've got."

Desmond took the spear, stepped to the edge of the cliff, and called out softly. "Lenny? Xavier?"

There was no answer.

He tried again, a bit louder. Still no response. He frowned and shook his head. After a moment, he took the spear and positioned it vertically over a spot that was covered in soil rather than bare rock. "Hold it here."

Infinity crawled to the spear and held it.

Desmond picked up a fist-sized rock and brought it down on

top of the spear. The weapon pierced the soil several inches. He hit it again, but the spear stopped, having obviously hit rock. He pulled it out and tried a different spot. It hit rock again. He moved it five feet back from the cliff's edge, but it still would go no more than a few inches before hitting the large sheet of rock beneath them.

They gazed at each other silently. One of them would have to lower the other down to the cave.

A shrill squawk broke the silence.

Infinity turned. A black bird man was coming up the hill straight for them, its tracking animal pulling frantically at its leash.

15

SURPRISE

Desmond was struggling to process the enormity of his mistake. Not only had his plan to reach the cave failed, but also he had led the black birds directly to Lenny and Xavier, if they were even still alive.

The creature and its tracking animal moved steadily up the hill. "I don't see the other one," Desmond said. "The two may have separated to find our trail after crossing the river. Maybe we can kill it."

Infinity grabbed his arm. "I can't fight. You need to run."

The bird man was just seconds away. Instead of arguing, Desmond ignored her instructions, grabbed the spear, and turned to face the creature. Infinity cursed and struggled to her feet. Unsteadily, she stood at Desmond's side, the stone knife in her hand.

The black bird stopped when its tracking animal was just out of the reach of Desmond's weapon. The six-foot bird man, still adorned with beaded cords around its body and limbs, gazed at them with black eyes and a face seemingly incapable of expression. Slowly, it removed the rope, crossbow, and knife hanging from its neck and tossed them on the ground, apparently wanting to fight with only its double-tipped spear. The bird man emitted a few soft whistles, and its tracking animal moved to the side, where it waited patiently.

"It's far more skilled than the brown birds," Infinity said. "Surprising it will be harder. But if you're not going to run, surprise is your only chance. I'm going to make it think I'm out of the fight." Suddenly she groaned and stumbled to the side. She dropped to her knees and collapsed onto her face, falling onto the crossbow the bird men had given them. She rolled to her side with her back to Desmond and the bird man.

"Infinity?"

She let out an exaggerated moan, followed by, "Keep him busy without getting yourself killed." These words came out as a continuous groan, as if she were in pain.

The creature stared at Infinity for a moment. Then it turned its attention back to Desmond. It held its spear out and shook it, apparently telling him to prepare to use his own spear. Desmond had the distinct impression the bird was growing impatient in its pursuit of an interesting challenge.

Aware that he was about to be painfully tormented again or even killed if he didn't get this right, he tried to think. Surprise. He had to surprise the bird man.

The black bird was now pacing, circling, waiting for him to make the first move.

What did Desmond know about these creatures? They had brought their young to watch forced combat, which had included the two-tipped spears each time. From the earliest age, these creatures learned the nuances of using these weapons. There was no way Desmond could beat this creature with a weapon it had probably been using all its life.

Abruptly, he stood up straight and shook his spear, mimicking the bird man's gesture. He tossed his spear to the ground. He pointed at it and then pointed at the spear in the bird man's hands. Then he crouched and held his bare hands out like a wrestler preparing to grapple.

The black bird stopped circling. It looked at the spear on the ground and back at Desmond.

"That's right," Desmond taunted. "You brave enough to fight without it?"

The bird man tossed its own spear aside. Without warning, it charged Desmond and tackled him, knocking him backward.

Desmond used the bird's momentum to roll it to the side. He managed to get on top of it and began frantically throwing punches, trying to overwhelm the bird with raw fury. He landed a couple of solid hits, but then the bird caught his left hand in its beak. It yanked his hand instantly to the side, nearly breaking the bones. It was on top of him before he knew what was happening.

Desmond tried getting ahold of the bird man's shoulder with his free hand, but only ended up coming away with a handful of feathers.

With Desmond's hand still gripped in its beak, the bird had two arms to fight with. It grabbed Desmond's free hand with one and shoved the other against Desmond's neck, its diminutive fingers clamping down on his throat.

Desmond tried pulling his left hand free, but the bird bit down harder, forcing him to cry out. The grip on his throat tightened, reducing his cry to a garbled choke.

This was it. The bird man was obviously done playing games.

Desmond tried to breathe but could only suck in tiny gasps.

The bird man gazed down at him silently, as if it were content to watch him slowly die.

Suddenly, he heard a snap. The bird man's head jerked to the side, it's beak releasing Desmond's hand as it groped at its own face. A foot-long arrow was protruding from the creature's eye.

The bird's grip on Desmond's throat loosened slightly, and he took a deep breath of air and twisted his head far enough to see Infinity. She was on her back. Her feet were in the air holding onto both arms of the crossbow. She was trying to extract a second arrow from the bottom of the weapon.

Desmond turned back to the bird man.

The creature was trying to pull the arrow from its head.

Desmond stretched his arm out to the side and then swung it as hard as he could, slamming his palm into the arrow's fletched end. This drove the arrow the rest of the way into the bird's head, and the tip came out through its other eye.

The creature squawked frantically, splattering Desmond's face with spittle, and it clamped its fingers harder on Desmond's throat. Blinded and enraged, it moved its other hand to Desmond's throat and began choking him with all its might.

"Goddammit!" he heard Infinity cry.

Desmond was busy trying to tear the bird's fingers from his throat, but he managed to crank his head to the side again. The tracking animal was attacking Infinity, going for her face. She had dropped the crossbow trying to fight it off.

Desmond let go of the bird man's fingers and reached across its face to grab the arrow protruding from its eye. He yanked on it, churning it back and forth in a desperate attempt to pulverize the contents of the creature's skull. But this was having little effect, and Desmond was starting to feel the prickly swelling of unconsciousness.

In a last-ditch effort, he twisted the arrow as hard as he could. Something gave way inside the bird's skull, and the arrow pivoted. The bird man went limp and collapsed on top of him.

He pushed the body to the side, rolled to his feet, and rushed over to Infinity.

Although twice the tracking animal's size, she was fighting for her life. The creature was relentlessly lunging at her, its beak now red from her blood. Her forearms were shredded from blocking its attacks.

Desmond grabbed the creature's leash and ran to the cliff, dragging the thrashing animal behind him. Without stopping, he swung it like a sack of rocks and launched it over the edge. Without emitting a single growl or squawk, the creature splashed into the river fifty feet below.

He ran back to Infinity and kneeled beside her. "Oh shit!"

"They're just minor cuts," she said, inspecting the wounds on her arms. "You're getting into the cave. Now." She crawled to the rope Desmond had dropped and gathered it up. "I'll lower you down."

"Give me that," he said. He took one end of the rope and tied it around the bird man's neck. He then extracted the other end from the coil and said, "Lift your arms." He began tying the other end around Infinity's chest above her breasts and under her armpits.

She said, "You can't go down last—that thing's body isn't heavy enough to hold your weight."

He finished tying the knot. "It'll work, trust me. Now, over the side." He grabbed the rope and sat at the cliff's edge with his feet braced.

A squawk came from lower on the hillside. They both turned to look. The other black bird and its tracking animal were running up the slope.

"Shit! Go!" he cried.

For a second she hesitated.

"There's no time to argue!" he shouted.

She rolled to her stomach and began sliding over the edge feet first. Her eyes met his. "I want you down there in twenty seconds." Then she was gone.

A large section of the rope slid through his hands, burning and scraping his palms. He tightened his grip, and her weight nearly pulled him over the side. He turned and looked down the slope. The bird man was halfway up the hill. It squawked again and released the leash. The tracking animal sprinted ahead. It would be on him in seconds.

The rope went slack. Infinity was in the cave.

Desmond frantically rolled onto his belly and pulled hand over hand on the extra loops of rope until he felt the tension of the black bird's carcass. Out of the corner of his eye he saw the tracking animal still charging at him. It was no more than twenty yards away. He skidded backward over the cliff's edge, putting all of his weight on the rope, just as the creature was closing the last few yards of distance. It opened its beak and lunged for his face as he cleared the edge, pulling the dead bird's body across the rocky ground above.

The carcass was lighter than he had thought, and he was sliding down the cliff face frighteningly fast. Just as the dark cave opening came into view, the black bird's body suddenly stopped sliding. Desmond lost his grip on the rope and began falling. Something gripped his ankle and pulled. He was slammed onto his back in the mouth of the cave. He rolled onto his side, trying to suck in air, the impact having knocked the wind from him.

Infinity released his ankle and frantically pulled at the rope, which was still tied around her chest. "The bastard's pulling me out!"

The rope was being pulled steadily up, lifting Infinity to her knees and then onto her feet. Still gasping for air, Desmond threw his arms around her legs just as her feet were lifted from the rock floor, holding her in place.

A few seconds later the rope slackened and Infinity dropped into a heap on top of Desmond. The rest of the rope was now dangling over the lip of the cave. It had broken or been cut.

Desmond was finally starting to get his breath back, and he sucked in huge lungfuls of air. Suddenly he remembered Lenny and Xavier, and he turned away from the cave opening. After his eyes adjusted, he saw that his friends were lying a few yards away at the back of the cave. They were both splotched with blood. And they weren't moving.

The cave ceiling sloped down sharply, so Desmond crawled to them. Xavier was sprawled on the cave floor in front of Lenny, with a blood-stained rock gripped in his hand. Desmond felt his face. It was warm. He pressed his ear to Xavier's chest and heard his heart beating. "Xavier!" He shook his shoulder.

Xavier sputtered, opened his eyes, and raised the rock as if he were going to swing it. "Desmond?"

"What happened here?" Desmond asked.

Xavier looked past Desmond at Infinity, and then he turned back to Desmond. He was obviously confused. "Birds. Big ones. They started showing up at sunset. I think they roost in here."

"They attacked you?"

Xavier nodded. "Big ones." He looked back at Lenny. "Oh, God, is he dead?"

Desmond leaned past Xavier and put a hand on Lenny's wrist. "No, he's alive."

"Twenty, maybe more," Xavier said. "Not happy we were here. They started attacking us. Never quit until morning. All night, they kept coming. Lenny lost consciousness after a few hours. I had to stay awake and fight them off. Otherwise they'd have torn him apart. They finally quit at daylight, and then I must have fallen asleep." He looked out the cave opening. "What time is it? How long until bridge-back?"

"We're getting close." Infinity said. She crawled back away from the cave's mouth. "Move aside, tourists. Let me examine him."

Desmond moved to the side.

With obvious effort, Xavier used his arms to move out of her way. Suddenly his eyes got wide. "What is that?"

Desmond turned. Suspended in the cave opening by a rope tied to one of its feet was the bird man's tracking animal. Before any of them could react, it was lowered to the cave floor, where it flipped over onto its feet and charged them.

Xavier was the closest, and he raised his rock to defend himself. But the creature grabbed his arm with its beak, and Xavier cried out in pain.

Immediately the rope tightened again, flipping the tracking animal upside down. It held on tightly to Xavier, and as the rope was pulled from above, the rising animal started dragging him to the mouth of the cave.

Desmond dove for the creature and managed to grab its free leg. He pulled down as hard as he could. The creature's bones cracked under his full weight. Astoundingly, it still didn't release Xavier's arm.

The creature kept rising, threatening to pull both Desmond and Xavier to the edge of the cave. The bird man above was stronger than Desmond had thought possible.

"It's breaking my arm!" Xavier cried.

Desmond's feet were now inches from the edge, and still the animal was being steadily pulled up. "Infinity, help!"

She stumbled forward and grabbed the tracking animal by the neck.

Xavier's eyes were desperate. "Careful, don't yank on it!"

With the weight of all three of them, the creature finally stopped rising. Suddenly the rope went slack, and Desmond, Xavier, Infinity, and the tracking animal collapsed to the floor in a writhing heap. Apparently the bird man above had decided to let go.

The creature's broken bones wouldn't allow it to get to its feet, but it flailed and scratched with its clawed forearms, still not releasing Xavier.

Infinity crawled away from the pile of bodies. "Use the rock!"

Desmond snatched the rock Xavier had dropped and began pummeling the creature's abdomen with it.

"Don't hit its head!" Xavier cried.

Desmond continued wildly pounding at the creature's body. But this was having no more effect than hitting the rubber dinosaur back at SafeTrek's training field. He noticed one of its ruined legs sprawled outward at an unnatural angle, so he slammed the rock on the knee joint, crushing the bones.

This time the creature let go. It lunged toward Desmond, its bloody beak gaping. Xavier was on his back but thrust his good foot, kicking the animal toward the cave opening. He scooted his body closer and kicked again, sending the creature over the edge to the river below.

For several seconds after the splash, nobody made any sounds except heavy breathing.

"The bastard still has one more rope," Infinity said eventually. "We have to expect him to use it."

Desmond scanned the cave's floor. He found a few more loose rocks small enough to pick up. He gave one to Xavier and one to Infinity, keeping the blood-soaked rock for himself. These were the only weapons they had.

"He's got the same problem we had," Desmond said. "Nothing to tie off to. Except his dead friend."

Infinity got to her feet, shaking and unsteady. "We're not underestimating it again. Get over here and get ready, both of you."

Xavier had been inspecting his arm, which looked pretty torn up, but now he stopped and stared up at her. "What's up there? Is it worse than the thing that just about broke my arm?"

She nodded. "Bigger, smarter, and highly skilled."

Xavier began pushing himself into position at her side. "This cave was supposed to be safe. It was the worst idea ever."

Desmond stepped to Infinity's other side. She was struggling to remain standing, and he worried she might fall over the edge. "Xavier," he said. "when you hear what we've been through, you may take that back. This is the safest place I've been since we bridged."

A sound came from above, like something heavy sliding over rock. A black body dropped into view, having kicked away from the cliff face just above the cave opening. It swung back in as it dropped, and then the black bird darkened the cave entrance as it landed on its feet before them. It released its rope from its beak just as the body of the other bird man fell past behind it.

Another splash came from below.

The bird man had a two-tipped spear in one hand and a stone knife in the other. It swiveled its head, taking in the scene, and then crouched low to the ground.

A thought ran through Desmond's mind—*If you're not going to run, surprise is your only chance.* Just as the bird man pushed off with one foot to attack, Desmond dove forward, driving his shoulder into the creature's chest before it could react.

He felt the bird man flailing in the air as they both fell from the cave. They fell forty feet in less than two seconds and hit the water. The bird man's back struck the riverbed, and Desmond's head slammed into its chest. Stunned, Desmond sucked water into his lungs. He coughed and sputtered, trying to get to his feet in the waist-deep water. When he finally stood up, he retched, spewing water from his lungs and esophagus.

The black bird rose to the surface beside him. The creature wasn't moving. Desmond grabbed one of its arms and flipped it over, face down. It began drifting away.

"Are you insane, Des?" It was Xavier's voice.

Still coughing, Desmond looked up. Infinity and Xavier were leaning out of the cave, watching him.

"Tourist, give me an injury report."

"I think... I'm okay."

"Good. Now, make sure that bastard is dead. Use a rock. Or hold its head under until you know."

The bird man was still face down, drifting slowly with the current. If it wasn't dead already, it would be drowned soon. Desmond stayed in place and counted to sixty, watching it float away. He decided that was long enough.

A carnivorous fish picked at his groin, and then several others began biting his legs. He made his way to the sand bar opposite the rock bluff. He turned to the west, where the sun was getting closer to the horizon. An hour until sunset, maybe two. Even though he was in an alternate universe, it was still August 4th here, and he was still in Missouri. It had to be close to 7:00 PM.

He looked downstream. The body of the first bird man—the one Desmond and Infinity had killed—had jammed up against a few boulders. The rope the second bird man had used would still be tied to the first. Desmond made his way along the sandbar to the body, waded out to the rope, and then pulled the body to shore. He looked at the dead creature and then up at the cave on the cliff face. The bird man was easily 150 pounds. It wouldn't be easy to drag, but there was nothing else up there to tie the rope to.

Desmond was already exhausted, and he was aware it would be easier just to find another place to hide. But at this moment he wanted to be up there with Infinity and Xavier and Lenny—perhaps more than anything he had ever wanted before. And what else was he going to do to kill the time? The thought of sitting alone somewhere in this hellish place for an hour or more without his friends was unbearable.

He began dragging the body downstream, limping and grunting from the effort and from the pain of his wounds.

Infinity called down to him—something about the stupidity of what he was doing. Xavier also said something, but Desmond was no longer listening. He pulled the body to the place where they had crossed the previous day. He waded across, ignoring the fish trying to feed on his skin. After pulling the body the rest of the way across, he tied the rope around his waist. He then turned around and leaned into it, slowly and painstakingly inching the bird's body up the sloped river-bank. When the body was on nearly-level ground, he turned and started walking upstream, dragging it between trees and over rocks and rotting logs. When he reached the base of the hill leading up to the top of the cliff, he stopped to rest. For a moment he thought he was still wet from the river, but he realized he was actually covered in his own sweat. He stood there, hands on his knees, until he had stopped wheezing. The rope was already rubbing skin off his waist, so he situated it a bit higher.

This entire grueling task had been a terrible idea. But he needed a purpose.

He started up the hill, dragging the body. The incline gradually increased, and soon he was pulling the body just a few inches at a time, resting between each effort while trying to prevent it from sliding back down.

Eventually, he emerged from the forest onto the open hillside. Now he could see the hill's summit, the place where they had killed the creature he was dragging. It wasn't far. But it seemed impos-sibly distant.

Lean and strain, dragging the body a few inches. Rest. Lean and strain. A few inches more. Rest.

He paused to look at the sun. How long had it been?

Abruptly, the sun and sky disappeared.

DESMOND LANDED ON HIS FEET, but then he collapsed onto his face, hitting the white, padded floor and leaving a splotch of blood and grime. Suddenly nauseous, he rolled to his side and cupped a hand over his mouth. A few seconds later, the urge to throw up passed.

"Severe injuries!" Infinity cried, her voice breaking and weak-ened. "First priority to Lenny. Unconscious from blood loss and possibly other factors. Bite wounds to his foot and ankle. Second priority, Xavier. Compound fracture, lower leg. Third priority, Desmond. Multiple stab wounds, broken nose, and possible internal injuries and shock from a forty-foot fall."

Desmond got to his knees as the airlock popped open and techs in white biosuits swarmed into the bridging room. Xavier was curled up on his side heaving, but nothing was coming out. Lenny was sprawled face down, motionless. A few feet away was a pile of black and red goo, pincushioned with splintered bones. Desmond stared at it, confused.

"It's best if you don't look at him," Infinity said.

He turned. She was sitting up, talking to him.

"We all bridge back, dead or alive," she said.

A gurney was wheeled in, and the techs lifted Lenny onto it and took him out. Another was brought in, and they lifted Xavier to his feet. As they helped him onto the gurney, his eyes met Desmond's.

"We made it back," Xavier said.

Desmond nodded.

The techs then wheeled Xavier out.

"Infinity, are you okay?" The voice was Armando Doyle's. It had come from speakers somewhere in the ceiling.

"I've been better."

"Can you walk on your own, sir?"

Desmond realized the tech beside him had spoken to him. "Yeah, I can walk."

"This way, then." The tech took him by the arm, helped him to his feet, and guided him toward the airlock.

"What in God's name happened?" Doyle asked.

"What the hell does it look like?" Infinity groaned as she got to her feet. "I'll tell you about it in the interview."

"How soon will you be ready?"

Desmond was almost through the first airlock door, but he stopped.

Infinity frowned and looked at Doyle through the window to the control room. "What's going on? I thought you weren't even going to be here?"

The tech pulled on Desmond's arm, but he refused to move. Something didn't seem right.

"I returned from California sooner than I had planned," Doyle said. "Something has changed. In fact, everything has changed."

16

INTERVIEW

Once the three tourists had been taken to the med lab, a tech brought in a gurney for Infinity. She had been injured on plenty of past excursions, but she had never allowed the techs to wheel her out of the bridging room. It hurt like hell to walk, and her pride had already been shredded anyway, so she accepted the help.

"Can you prioritize your injuries, Infinity?" The question came from the med tech, a woman named Poppy Safran. Poppy was the first to examine Infinity after every bridge-back.

Infinity gently touched her right hip. "This is the worst. Arrow went all the way through. I don't even know if the bone is intact."

Poppy poked at the entrance wound, examining it. "You tried to plug this?"

"A mud plug."

Behind her biosuit faceplate, Poppy shook her head. "Jesus, Infinity." She reached for the handle of the digital X-ray machine mounted to the ceiling and pulled it down and into place above Infinity's hip. "Let's take a quick look. We'll take more detailed X-rays later—I know Armando needs to talk to you ASAP." She loosened a knob on the flat X-ray detector positioned beneath the table and moved it into place beneath Infinity's hip. "Hold your breath, hon." She tapped the touchscreen display a few times and stared at the resulting image. "Can you roll onto your left side?"

Infinity complied. "What's up with Armando?"

"I'd better let him explain. Don't breathe." She took another image.

Infinity didn't like the sound of that. "Explain what?"

Poppy studied the image, ignoring the question. "I don't see any fractures or chipping. From what I can tell, the object just missed the femoral head, maybe by only a few millimeters. If it had damaged your femoral head, you wouldn't be walking at all. I'd say you were lucky—as usual."

"Good to know. Explain *what*, Poppy?"

Poppy gazed at her through the biosuit's faceplate. "If this is the worst of your injuries, you'll be moving around like normal in a few weeks. Which is good, because we need you."

Infinity frowned and studied Poppy's face. The med tech wasn't acting like herself. She was nervous, blinking frequently, and perspiring, even though her biosuit was cooled. "I was thinking of taking some time off," Infinity said. "This excursion was a goddamn disaster. Maybe I'm even done for good."

Poppy pursed her lips and shook her head. She was actually trembling. "No, Infinity, you're not."

Twenty minutes later, Poppy put Infinity in a wheelchair and took her to the interview chamber. Infinity had been shot up with antibiotics as well as a moderate stimulant to help her get through the interview. A gel pack had been taped to each of her wounds, which meant about 40% of her body was now covered in tape.

Poppy opened the chamber door and wheeled her in. The room was actually part of the sealed bridging recovery area, so there was no need for an airlock here. Poppy positioned Infinity and her wheelchair behind the waist-high concealment barrier. The tech then unfolded a sterile paper gown and handed it to Infinity.

"What the hell is this?" Infinity asked.

"Armando told us to make an exception this time. You might want to cover up." She stepped to the door, but then she turned back to gaze at Infinity, creases etched into the skin on the sides of her mouth. "Infinity, I've always admired you. You're the best bridger we have. Thank you."

This strange statement was further evidence that something was happening, but Infinity was too exhausted to try extracting more information from Poppy. She would be in the loop soon enough. Before Poppy shut the door, Infinity said, "Where's the tourist, Desmond? He's well enough to be here for the interview, isn't he?"

"I think he is. But we thought you might want to do it without—"

"I want him here."

She nodded. "I'll see what I can do."

Several minutes later, Poppy brought Desmond in, also in a wheelchair, and parked him beside Infinity.

"Thank you, Poppy," Infinity said.

The med tech gave her a smile, but it was obviously forced. She then stepped out and closed the door.

Infinity looked Desmond up and down. Like her, he was covered in taped-on gel packs. A paper gown, still folded, lay in his lap. "Your friends doing okay?" she asked.

He shook his head. "I don't know. They took them both straight to surgery. Lenny might lose his foot."

"He won't. We've got good people here."

He nodded and then glanced around the room. "I don't know these people like you do, but they're acting kind of—"

The room behind the plexiglass window lit up abruptly as

someone turned on the lights. Armando stepped into the room. Behind him came three more men, all in white shirts and ties— probably academics, although two of them seemed unusually lean and attentive. The third, an older man, looked familiar to Infinity. Had she seen him in the interview room before?

She sensed the tourist tensing up beside her and frowned at him.

He shot her a glance. "What's going on? Why is Morgan Macpherson here?"

She looked through the window again as the men took their seats. Why did that name sound familiar? She turned back to the tourist, shaking her head. "Who?"

"Morgan Macpherson. The vice president of the United States?"

She turned back to the window. "Oh, shit."

Macpherson raised his brows, and Armando said, "The mic is on, Infinity."

She swallowed. She had thought she was prepared for about anything. But something was seriously wrong.

Vice President Macpherson leaned forward in his chair. "Miss Fowler, first I'd like to say I'm sorry about the unfortunate loss of your partner."

Infinity snatched the paper gown Poppy had left and draped it over her chest. "But," she said, "that's not why you're here."

"No, it's not. I addressed the other SafeTrek bridgers earlier today. But I wanted to stay here until your return so I could talk to you personally. My purpose here is to lend credibility and gravitas to what you are about to hear. President Millwright would be here herself if it were possible."

Infinity felt like she was in a freakish dream. "I'm listening."

"SafeTrek is no longer a private company. Its operation is now administered by the federal government."

"What? Since when?"

Armando raised his hands. "Listen, Infinity. This is something we're cooperating with completely." He glanced at Macpherson. "Do you mind if I explain?"

The vice president nodded. "By all means."

Armando gazed at Infinity and Desmond through the transparent barrier. He was more disheveled than usual. His hair was hardly combed, and his eyes were red, perhaps from lack of sleep. Even his bow tie was missing. And he had that same strained look Infinity had seen on Poppy's face. He cleared his throat and shifted in his chair. "A lot has happened in the last thirty-six hours. I understand you were told before bridging yesterday that the Allen Telescope Array had picked up another radio signal, from a second alien civilization."

Desmond said, "We were told about the new signal, but it was uncertain whether the signal was from a second civilization."

"That is no longer an uncertainty," the vice president said.

Infinity and Desmond exchanged a glance. "What confirmed that?" he asked.

Armando went on. "As you've been told, upon learning of the second signal, I immediately flew to Mountain View to join the discussions at the SETI Institute. Obviously I have a vested interest in the implications. I thought I might participate in sorting out the transmitted information. Since this signal used the same formatting protocols as the first, the content had already been revealed by the time I arrived. The source is slightly under 42 degrees of arc from the Outlanders, from our perspective. Preliminary estimates suggest the source could be as far as 3,000 parsecs from the Outlander source—almost 10,000 light years."

Infinity was getting tired of all this beating around the bush. "Maybe you could just tell us what the hell's going on."

Armando frowned. But then he nodded. "The signal came from a source far from that of the original signal, but that's not how we know it's from a different civilization. Listen carefully, kiddo."

Infinity blinked at him. He had never called her that in front of a tourist. She gritted her teeth and nodded.

"We know it's from a different civilization because it contains a warning."

Desmond said it first—"A warning?"

"Apparently we aren't the only civilization to receive and decode the Outlander signal. At some point in the past, this second civilization received it as well. And they constructed bridging devices, just as we have done. Soon after starting to use the devices, they began observing unusual weather events. And their planet's surface became unstable."

Infinity glanced at Desmond. His face was pale.

The vice president said, "We now believe that we understand what is happening to our own planet."

"And what is that?" Infinity asked.

"The bridging devices," Armando said. "Each time they are used, they create a handful of some kind of particle we have never encountered before. Previously, we had no way to detect these particles. We suspect the second alien civilization was more technologically advanced than we are, but the signal they transmitted made it clear they did not fully understand the process whereby the particles were being created. But what they did understand is more than enough. The content of their signal is detailed and very convincing."

Armando paused, and a lump began forming in Infinity's throat. She sensed everything was about to change—and not in a good way. Armando was looking at her like a father would look at a daughter before explaining he was dying of cancer.

"The second signal described the particles generated by the bridging device as having two properties. First, they consume every other particle they touch. More accurately, every particle they touch disappears. In the same way your hair disappears when you bridge. No idea where it goes—probably to another universe. The second property is that the particles are heavy. Once they're created, they immediately begin falling to the planet's center of gravity. Every particle in their path disappears. They pass through the planet's core and continue on until gravity pulls them back to the core again. The result is that all of these new particles gradually accumulate at the earth's center."

"And there they sit, eating away at the core," Desmond added. "As the core becomes smaller, the earth's crust is destabilized."

Armando nodded. "Earthquakes, extreme weather events, disruption of the magnetosphere. Which is why we're seeing auroras over Missouri."

Infinity was beginning to understand what the tourist had apparently already figured out. "You're saying this is going to get worse?"

Armando nodded again. "The second alien civilization was convinced their planet's complete destruction was inevitable. They constructed a transmitter for their signal on a craft in orbit around their dying planet. We assume that eventually the craft was released from the diminishing gravitational pull as their planet was reduced to nothing. Then it probably drifted off through space, still transmitting its signal."

Several seconds of silence followed.

"So the second signal was sent out as a warning," Desmond said.

"Yes," Armando replied. "Likely with the hope that other civilizations would discover the warning before discovering the original signal, and would avoid creating and using the bridging devices. Unfortunately, we discovered the original signal first."

Desmond grabbed the concealment barrier with both his hands. "It doesn't make sense! Why would an intelligent civilization send out blueprints for a technology that destroys planets?"

"It makes perfect sense," Infinity said. "It's a Trojan horse. A weapon. Or more accurately, a deadly lure. I know you people want to believe alien civilizations are naturally friendly, but there is no strategic advantage to being friendly. And there's definitely no advantage to giving away critical technology. You know what *does* give a civilization strategic advantage? Destroying every other civilization that could someday become a threat. And what makes even more sense is to develop an inexpensive, efficient way to do that. A way that allows you to sit back on your ass as every developing civilization close enough to become a threat receives your radio signal and eagerly destroys itself. The signal is a lure. And those bastards knew no one could resist the lure of infinite universes."

Again several seconds of silence followed.

Desmond released the barrier and leaned back. "Is it too late to stop the process?"

The vice president said, "We have no idea, but we have to assume it is."

"How much time do we have?" Infinity asked.

"Again," the vice president said, "we have no idea."

She looked from the vice president to Armando, and then back to the vice president. "The planet is being destroyed, and you came here to talk to us in person? You could have given the order to quit using the bridging device over the phone. Why are you here?"

The vice president nodded. "Because we don't want you to quit using the device."

She glanced at Armando, but his face was like a stone.

Macpherson went on. "The United States government does not have a contingency plan for this. We have strategies for everything else you can imagine, including an impending asteroid impact. But all of those plans involve seeking shelter on a traumatized earth. None of them involve an earth that ceases to exist. And we are decades from having the capability to move even a few people off the planet. To put it simply, if the second alien signal's prediction proves to be correct, the human species is screwed."

Infinity's mind raced as she began to realize why the vice president had come to SafeTrek. But what he wanted was impossible. "You want to bridge people to another world, don't you? Do you have any goddamn idea how—"

"Infinity!" It was Armando. "Vice President Macpherson is aware of the limitations of bridging. Hear him out."

Macpherson cleared his throat. "For the time being, we must assume the threat is real. All evidence matches what we have deciphered from the second radio signal. Perhaps in the coming weeks —assuming the earth exists that long—we'll know more. But in the meantime, if there is any chance of preventing the total extinction of the human race, we must take it. That's why I'm here. We need good bridgers. We need you to find suitable worlds. When you do, we'll have carefully-selected groups of people here ready to bridge to those worlds. And then—"

Infinity stopped him with a raised palm. "Listen! It takes thirty-six hours to do a bio-probe. If the bio-probe is successful, it takes thirty-six hours to send bridgers to check it out. We have access to each alternate world for only 108 hours. That leaves only thirty-six hours before we lose access to that world forever."

Armando spoke up. "Again, we're all aware of the limitations. We've never bridged more than five people at once, but there is no reason we can't bridge more than that—perhaps even thirty at once. And we think we can have the bridging device up to full power and ready again within an hour of each bridging. Infinity, I believe we can bridge about a thousand people to a specific world within thirty-six hours."

Infinity stared in disbelief. This was their plan to save the human species?

"I want to be a part of this," the tourist said.

Everyone turned to him.

He glanced nervously at Infinity and then addressed the men behind the plexiglass window. "You need bridgers, and I've had some experience now. I want to help."

Infinity gazed at him. For some reason, at that moment, it actually hit her that the world was ending. Everyone was going to die except for a few who were bridged to alternate universes. Only seven bridging facilities existed on Earth. How many was it even possible to save? Each thousand who were bridged to an alternate world would need skilled guides to help them survive and start a colony. Infinity was damn sure she would not be among those selected to survive unless she were one of the guides.

Armando said, "One excursion could hardly be considered experience, Mr. Weaver."

"He can be my partner," Infinity blurted out.

Now everyone turned to her.

"He saved my life. Not only that, but he has the ability to recall long strings of information, a skill that could be highly useful. He'll make a damn good bridger." She turned to Armando. "If you want me in on this insane plan, Desmond's going to be my partner."

EXTINCTION

August 19 (fifteen days later)

THE SUBTLE SHAKING of another tremor broke Desmond's concentration, resulting in a jab to his gut from Infinity's double-tipped, four-foot spear.

"You took your eyes off mine again," she said. "Watch my face, not my weapon. Look at me!"

Desmond stared at her.

She jiggled the rubber tip of her spear up and down. "Can you see what my weapon is doing while you're looking at my eyes?"

He sighed. "Yes."

"Of course you can. Now watch my eyes." After a few seconds she narrowed them slightly and tightened her mouth, and a split second later she thrust the spear.

This time he blocked it.

She nodded. "That's better."

Desmond held one hand up and stepped over to the picnic table to get a drink. He checked the time on his phone. "We've been at this for three hours. Take a break with me." They had done half-hour drills with six different weapons, and the training yard behind the SafeTrek building was starting to heat up under the late-morning sun.

She shrugged and joined him at the picnic table. They both drank deeply from their water bottles. For several minutes they sat on the table listening to the murmur of activity from the sprawling acres of lawn and forest on the front side of the SafeTrek building. A few weeks ago, the SafeTrek building had been hidden away, isolated at the end of a half-mile private road running through mature Missouri oak-hickory forest. Now, the area on either side of that road had been cleared to make room for almost 2,000 living spaces, including RVs, bunkhouse trailers, and wall tents. There was enough temporary housing to accommodate 1,436 refugees—two groups of 718 people selected to bridge permanently to alternate worlds. In addition, the encampment was occupied by another 600 people: 100 security officers, 300 workers responsible for providing food, sanitary services, medical treatment, and last-minute survival training to the refugees, and another 200 spouses and children of these workers. The workers and their families had been promised a place in the last group to bridge, as long as they continued providing their services until that day came. And since it was becoming clearer every day that the earth was indeed dying—and dying fast—all of the workers were diligently committed to their duties.

Any of the bridgers surviving until then would be allowed to go with the last group.

Someone at the federal level had decided there needed to be age restrictions for colony members, due to the potential hardships. In spite of the resulting public outcry, no one under fifteen or over sixty could participate. Whether this rule was right or wrong, it had reduced the once-overwhelming number of people demanding spots in the colonies. The only families eligible were those with all members between the fifteen to sixty slot.

Through frantic trial and error at the seven bridging facilities around the world, it had been discovered that one-way, non-return bridging could be accomplished by simply not administering the radioisotope marker. It had also been shown that about twenty-three people could bridge at one time, presumably limited by total biomass. And so the agreed-upon safe standard was twenty people. Lastly, it had been proven that bridging devices could consistently be made ready for bridging another group fifty-two minutes after the previous bridge, so sixty minutes was considered a safe standard. This allowed 718 refugees, plus two bridgers, to be bridged in the available thirty-six hours. So 718 had become the standard population size for each new human colony. Although there were seven bridging facilities, only five colonies had so far been bridged to other versions of Earth. This was due to a number of failed bio-probes and world-assessment excursions. The SafeTrek facility had bridged one of those five.

The back door to the building popped open abruptly. Lenny came out, followed by Xavier, each of them on crutches with one leg in a cast from the knee down. Behind them came a woman and man Desmond hadn't seen before.

"You two are hardcore," Lenny said as he propped his crutches against the picnic table and sat down. "It's freaking sweltering out here."

"Yeah, it's hard to stay hydrated," Desmond said. "Couple of weeks and you two will be training out here with us."

"That might be pushing it," Xavier said. "We'll be ready when we're ready." He turned to the man and woman behind him. "Lorissa and Zachariah, meet your bridgers, Decay and Infinity. Decay and Infinity, meet Lorissa and Zachariah, your tourists. Or environment evaluators, or whatever we're calling them now.

Lenny and I are giving them the grand tour, seeing as we're not good for much else around here."

Desmond appraised the tourists as he shook their hands. "You don't have to call me Decay. Just call me Desmond." He estimated they were both in their forties. The woman appeared to be in decent physical shape. The man, on the other hand, was slightly pudgy and didn't look like he spent much time in the sun.

As Desmond had expected, Infinity stayed put, not interested in shaking hands.

But Lorissa stepped around the picnic table and extended a hand to her anyway. "I'm from the University of Oklahoma. Agricultural sciences."

"And I'm at Iowa State," Zachariah said. "Microbiology and Parasitology."

Infinity nodded. She shook Lorissa's extended hand but didn't reply to either of them.

Zachariah slapped his hands together. "My goodness! Real bridgers, in the flesh. If we weren't meeting under such dire circumstances, this would all be downright exhilarating."

Finally, Infinity spoke. "By *dire*, you mean everyone on Earth will be dead soon?"

The guy frowned. "Well, yes. I suppose. I was just trying to impose some levity."

Infinity gave no response.

Lenny cleared his throat. "Well, damn. As far as awkward moments go, I'd give that one a seven."

Desmond spoke to Lenny and Xavier, "I suppose this means Wraith and Trencher have had a successful bio-probe?" Wraith and Trencher were the bridgers up for the next excursion. If they returned with positive news, SafeTrek's second group of 718 refugees would bridge.

"Yep, the bio-probe came back two hours ago," Xavier said. "Lenny and I were there to see it return. Every test animal alive but one. So Doyle asked us to bring Lorissa and Zach to meet you. You're supposed to start their training today."

Again, Desmond appraised the tourists. So this was really happening—he and Infinity would be next in line.

Lorissa spoke up. "According to protocol, our group has voted on which divergence point to select for our new home. The overwhelming majority of us would prefer a world without other humans. We would like to have our own identity as we begin a new human colony, rather than simply melding into an existing population. So we have chosen a divergence point of 210,000 years."

This plan made sense to Desmond. *Homo sapiens* had shown up on Earth about 195,000 years ago. Since most evolutionary events were random and unlikely, in a do-over of the last 210,000 years, humans probably wouldn't even appear at all.

Lenny grabbed his crutches and struggled to his feet. "Wraith and Trencher will be back in less than thirty-six hours, probably with news of a suitable world. So they'll have thirty-six hours to bridge 718 lucky bastards." He turned to Desmond. "And then we'll initiate *your* bio-probe—another thirty-six hours. So my wicked-keen mathematical mind figures you've got 108 hours until pucker time." He looked at Lorissa and Zachariah. "Sorry, but the fun part of your tour is over."

Xavier nudged Zachariah's shoulder. "Might as well take your clothes off now. Your training doesn't get *real* until you do."

He and Lenny turned and crutched their way back toward the air-conditioned SafeTrek building.

———

DESMOND COULDN'T SLEEP, which had become a nightly problem during the last two weeks. When he did sleep, he often dreamed of his mom, huddled up in her home in Lexington as horrifying, inescapable earthquakes or tsunami waves devastated everything around her. He sighed, pushed the covers off, and sat up in his bed, rubbing his eyes in frustration. His mom was over sixty, therefore not allowed to join a colony. He got up and pulled on a pair of shorts, left his bunk room, and padded barefoot down the SafeTrek halls to the metal door leading to the training field in the back. He smiled when he saw the door had been propped open with a small rock. All doors were kept locked now, and the rock meant Infinity wasn't sleeping either.

He emerged under a starry, moonless sky. He was slightly disappointed that no aurora was visible. He stood still for a minute or so, letting his eyes adjust to the darkness. Even as late as it was, a considerable amount of noise filtered around the building, including what sounded like someone wailing in anguish. Seven hundred and eighteen of the refugees would soon leave this world forever. Everyone had their own way of dealing with such knowledge. Several days earlier, Desmond had made the mistake of wandering through the makeshift village of waiting refugees. Most of them seemed to be living their last hours on this world in a sedative-induced daze, walking a fine line between euphoria and emotional breakdown. Even though they were fortunate to have been selected, they would soon leave everything they had ever known for an existence filled with hardships they could barely fathom.

Infinity was sitting on the picnic table. Her skin glistened in the starlight, probably from holding yoga poses Desmond couldn't come close to replicating.

She glanced at him as he sat on the tabletop beside her, but she didn't say anything. She turned her gaze upward again, and they stared silently at the stars.

"It's almost cold out here," Desmond muttered. It wasn't actually cold, but he thought this half-joking hint might make her smile.

She nodded slightly. Then she surprised him by turning toward him. "Scoot your ass back."

He moved back from the edge of the table to make room for her. She sat between his legs and leaned back against his chest. The two weeks of hair growth on her scalp felt soft on his skin.

Several minutes passed.

"At least we don't have to worry about falling out of a tree this time," he said.

She didn't reply.

"You feel like talking?" he asked.

"Not really. But that won't stop you, will it?"

He blew out a one-huff laugh. "I've been thinking about this whole effort. I know the idea is to save the human species from extinction. But humans still exist in an infinite number of other universes, so does it really matter?"

She shrugged. "No one wants to die. So we fight to stay alive."

"But it's not like our species would really go extinct, right?"

"I don't know. One time Armando tried explaining parallel universes to me, although I'm pretty sure he doesn't know that much about the subject. Those universes we bridge to? I guess they don't actually exist until we bridge there—until we observe them."

Desmond tried unsuccessfully to grasp this concept. "That's messed up. And it's why I'm a biologist, not a physicist."

"Each universe is just the result of a different version of our own history. Armando has a favorite quote: 'We create history by observing it, rather than history creating us.'"

He sighed loudly and decided to change the subject. "I called my mom again today."

"Yeah?"

"She's handling all this pretty well. I told her I won't give up on trying to get her an exemption on the age restriction. But she said it's okay, as long as *I* get to go." He shook his head. "She's always been that way."

Infinity didn't respond, and Desmond realized he may have said the wrong thing.

"My dad died when I was five," he said. "Are your parents still living?"

She shrugged slightly. "No idea."

He decided he'd better not push it. He looked down at her hand resting on his knee. The faded SafeTrek tattoo was barely visible. Desmond glanced at his own SafeTrek tattoo on the back of his right hand. His was fresh. When he had officially been designated a bridger, Infinity had insisted he get the tattoo. All the SafeTrek bridgers had them. One of the med techs was an amateur tattoo artist and did them for free. Desmond put his hand on the painted bunting tattoo on her chest, which was definitely not done by an amateur. "You going to try to get this re-inked one last time before our final bridge?"

"Too late. My artist left for Texas to be with his kids. Besides, I doubt there will be a final bridge."

"Why do you say that?"

She tilted her head forward and then back, thumping his chest like this was a stupid question. "Think about it. Our job is to find good worlds for each refugee group. SafeTrek is going to keep bridging new groups off this world until the last minute. Which will probably be when the generators give out or the building collapses in an earthquake. Chances are, that'll happen during a bio-probe or while refugees are being bridged. Where does that leave you and me?"

He removed his hand from her tattoo. "Thanks for cheering me up."

She thumped his chest again. "Well, here's the way I look at it. For the first time in my life, I'm with someone I don't mind dying with. And I'll take that."

AUTHOR'S NOTES

This story is based on the rather mind-bending concept of the possible existence of infinite parallel universes.

While there are certainly cosmologists who are skeptical of the concept, it is important to point out that multiple parallel universes is not a *theory*. Scientists did not simply come up with the idea using their imaginations. Instead, the concept is a mathematical consequence of our current theories in physics, particularly *quantum mechanics* and *string theory*. What this means, essentially, is that even those physicists who are skeptical of the idea must examine it as a real possibility (even if they do so reluctantly).

If we assume that quantum mechanics and string theory are not completely wrong, then it is important for scientists to examine all of the mathematical consequences of those theories. Even if those consequences (such as parallel universes) seem strange to us.

There are at least five plausible scientific theories that suggest the existence of multiple universes (the "multiverse"). My favorite of these is the concept of "daughter universes" suggested by the theory of quantum mechanics. Quantum mechanics describes things in terms of probabilities, rather than definite outcomes. The mathematics of quantum mechanics suggest that every possible outcome of every situation actually occurs—in its own separate universe.

Everything is made up of tiny particles, and what this "daughter universes" concept boils down to is that there could be infinite parallel universes, each of them differing by the position of only one particle.

The concept boggles the mind. But it certainly makes for a fun story.

Okay, so what about the idea of a world inhabited by large birds rather than large mammals? This is not as far-fetched as you might think. Sixty-six million years ago, the massive K-T extinction occurred as a result of an asteroid striking the earth. About 75% of all plant and animal species went extinct, including the non-avian dinosaurs (avian = bird-like).

However, the bird-like dinosaurs persisted. They evolved into the 10,000 or more bird species alive today. And some small species of mammals persisted. They evolved into the 5,400 species of mammals alive today. Sure, there are currently more birds than mammals, but mammals have filled most of the large-bodied carnivore and herbivore niches.

It's not unreasonable to imagine that, in a do-over of the K-T extinction, those small mammals may not have made it. This definitely was a possibility. And if those mammals had gone extinct along with the non-avian dinosaurs, it is likely that the bird-like dinosaurs would have eventually filled the large-bodied carnivore and herbivore niches.

Would some of those birds have eventually become intelligent? I guess we'll never know. Unless we someday develop a bridging device so that we can look at the results of numerous do-overs of the K-T extinction. In the meantime, I find it fun to speculate.

ACKNOWLEDGMENTS

I am not capable of creating a book such as this on my own. I have the following people, among others, to thank for their assistance.

When it comes to editing, my son Micheal Smith is extremely talented, and his tireless and meticulous suggestions are invaluable. If you find a sentence or detail in the book that doesn't seem right, it is likely because I failed to implement one of his suggestions.

My wife Trish is always the first to read my work, and therefore she has the burden of seeing my stories in their roughest form. Thankfully, she does not hesitate to point out where things are a mess. Her suggestions are what get the editing process started. She also helps with various promotional efforts. And finally, she not only tolerates my obsession with writing, she actually encourages it.

I also owe thanks to those on my Advance Reviewer team. They pointed out numerous typos and inconsistencies. Several went above and beyond, including Mandy Walkden-Brown, Sherri Rusch, Tammy Chambers, Lisa Ensign, Ilene Roberts, Linda Gray, Jack Waddington, Bridgit Davis, and Jenny Avery.

Finally, I am thankful to all the independent freelance designers out there who provide quality work for independent authors such as myself. Jake Caleb Clark (www.jcalebdesign.com) created the awesome cover for *Bridgers 1: The Lure of Infinity*. Najla (najlakay on fiver.com) created the cool map in the front matter of the book.

ABOUT THE AUTHOR

Stan Smith has lived most of his life in the Midwest United States and currently resides in Warrensburg, Missouri. He writes adventure novels and short stories that have a generous sprinkling of science fiction. His novels and stories are about regular people who find themselves caught up in highly unusual situations. They are designed to stimulate your sense of wonder, get your heart pounding, and keep you reading late into the night, with minimal risk of exposure to spelling and punctuation errors. His books are for anyone who loves adventure, discovery, and mind-bending surprises.

Stan's Author Website
http://www.stancsmith.com

Feel free to email Stan at: stan@stancsmith.com
He loves hearing from readers and will answer every email.

THERE'S MORE TO THIS STORY

Infinity and Desmond are just getting started—there's so much work to be done. Be sure to check out the next book in the series:

Bridgers 2: The Cost of Survival

How far would you go to save the human species?

Heart to blood, muscle to bone, tourist flesh above my own. It's the bridgers' directive: risk your own life to save tourists bridging to alternate worlds. Bridger Infinity Fowler has no qualms about the directive. Risking death is just what bridgers do. But now the earth is dying. Bridgers have a new directive—save as many humans as possible, even if some must be sacrificed in the process. Sacrificing lives is not what Infinity signed up for.

Desmond Weaver, determined to help save the human species, has volunteered to be Infinity's partner. He has ingenuity and grit, but is this enough to make it as a bridger?

Their mission: bridge 718 refugees to a new world and establish a colony. If the world is occupied, avoid conflict and learn to coexist.

Once bridging begins, there is no turning back. The new world is indeed occupied, but not by humans, and avoiding conflict isn't so easy. As violence erupts, Infinity and Desmond realize they may have only one hope of saving the colony—sacrificing refugees they have sworn to protect.